THE WHITE WITCHES AND THEIR NINE PRECIOUS JEWELS

Book 2 – The Magic Diamond of Lucas Cave

S.E.Aitken

DEDICATION

This book is dedicated to everyone who needs to escape from the world for a short time, and to my loving family, Talia, Ricky, Niall, Bex, Elvy-Rose, Baby McMillan, Stanley, Nikita, Jolina, My Late Mother (who was never a big fan of my Pixies), Dad-(I hope you can now see, it is actually okay to live in 'Cloud Cuckoo Land'), Tina, Craig, Joy, Gran, Gordon and all of you who will become part of our family of enormous hearts'

ACKNOWLEDGMENTS

A big thank you to my beta readers and editors who did an amazing job

Thank you to Andea Orlic for the outstanding cover design (once again)

Thank you to Talia McMillan and Niall Highton, my children who always stand in my corner

Contents

CHAPTER 1

THE WEDDING

D o you think she knows?' Emerald said, neck strained swan like around the doorway at the foot of the stairs, eager to start a conversation

The house was in almost complete silence except for the rhythmic sound of the grandmother clock, kicking away the seconds. Ruby watched the rise and fall of her granddaughter Primroses chest satisfying herself that she was comfortable in her bed, whilst gently closing her bedroom door. She knew she had become too old for the nightly check-ins at the age of thirteen, but it was a hard habit to break. Tentatively placing a tattered slipper flatly on the densely carpeted staircase, she tiptoed downstairs.

'I know she doesn't' Ruby said in a hushed voice placing a crinkly figure on her lips in the hope the gesture would lower the decibels in Emerald's voice as she squeezed past her in the doorway.

'I think she knows something. She knows she is different than other girls her age.' Sapphire muttered taking a slurp of wine from the hand warmed goblet which she had been nursing for the past hour.

'You may be right but, Buttercup said she would only tell her when she felt she was old enough to understand. Revealing it to her now would be to go against her mother's wishes and Buttercup can be pretty darn scary if you get on the wrong side of her.'

'Paha' Sapphire scoffed almost spraying the multi coloured patchwork sofa with red wine as she spoke.

'She needs to be told, and QUICKLY. The girl is thirteen and the spell will wear off soon. Validor and the human world will be at risk again. Have you forgotten what happened last time?' Her eyes now widened with concern. Ruby winced and gave a tight plain smile, unthankful for the unfiltered reminder. *She remembered it very well. How could she possibly forget ......?*

♟♟♟

Beads of sweat escaped from Charles's forehead as he awaited Amber's answer. He furiously mopped his brow with a dirty white handkerchief hastily retrieved from his trouser pocket. His chest still carrying the weight of many years of loneliness. A weight that could only be diminished by hearing one word. A small, but so very big word to him. *Please say yes, please say yes.* Perhaps by willing Amber's response in his mind, a miracle may occur. He could not be sure, but it was worth a try. The answer Amber gave at this very moment would change his life forever. For better or for worse. Her hands wrung

2

together, and her throat quivered as she swallowed and began to respond. Charles now unsettled by the fact that he was surrounded by so many people who could witness what may become his own humiliation and heartbreak, but it was a small price to pay. Their bodies were still in the form of animated tiny lights floating in the air, (the remains of Pearls prior spell used to transport them to the White Witch Coven). He wondered, *how does her face look. Is she happy or filled with pity, or perhaps she was finding it too difficult to force out the painful truth? Say something please Amber.*

'Yes Charles-Yes I will marry you!' Amber whispered quietly. She felt very conscious of the number of eyes on her in the room and wanted to escape them as quickly as she could even more unsettling was the fact that they were invisible to her. Charles's danced around as a bead of light, moving up and down like notes on a sheet of music.

'WAIT, WAIT!' Screamed Moonstone flying in her usual apologetic, clumsy way across the palace courtyard and inadvertently making physical contact with each person as she passed. 'Sorry. Ooops, Sorry!'

Pearls light bounced next to her in a feverish and angry pattern.

'What is it Moonstone? Settle down! This is not an appropriate moment to interrupt!'

'Pearl, your timing is perfect as always, or maybe not so perfect as you failed to see the importance of this. I think you should change us all back to the physical form until we leave Validor. It looks like we have a wedding to attend, and poor Charles has not seen his bride to be for so many years!'

Pearl bounced into Moonstone's light as if to say *be quiet.*

'Of course, I was about to make the change. Be patient. Lightania, Menanca, Portaya!' She bellowed in a deep husky voice.

Pearl appeared first with a pop. She looked at her arms and feet as if checking whether she might be missing a limb or article of clothing. Next it was Moonstone. Pop. Her feet now teetering on top of Pearls almost crushing them into what might become feet sized breadcrumbs.

'Move your feet clumsy!' said Pearl, smashing a dainty white porcelain shoulder into Moonstone. Moonstone stumbled trying to regain her footing.

Pearl did not like to be close to people literally or metaphorically especially not Moonstone. Amber crashed to the floor ungracefully next to a bewildered Charles, then, in unison their heads swing around, now meeting one another's love-struck gaze, they wrapped their arms tightly around each other, holding each other's face in their hands, forehead to forehead not quite believing what they were seeing.

'You look just like I remember. I missed you so much!' Charles sighed.

'I missed you too Charles, it feels like a lifetime since I last saw you'

'It is a lifetime, but it is not over yet. We have so many happy years to look forward to!'

Ruby rolled around the stone floor, puffing and panting. Alex squirmed on top of her, flapping around, kicking his legs like a fish out of water.

'So sorry Ruby' he blushed his face glowing crimson red.

'No problem Alex. It was not your fault'. She began brushing the creases of her skirt and guided her fingers through her tangled hair. Her eyes fixed rigidly to the floor. Pearl raised a suspicious eyebrow; *Alex is not to be trusted remember Pearl* she thought. Then immediately shifted her gaze to the floor. *Snap out of it.*

Morganite stumbled to a standing position. Dusting down his pristine loose white pants.

'Totally undignified. Pearl, you must find a way to make this a little more, well, elegant. I don't mean to criticize but'

'Well don't then. Simple?' She hissed.

'OH touchy. Get over yourself Pearl' Sapphire chuckled, slapping Pearl on the back, trying to lighten the mood.

'You really need to lighten up! Pearl jolted forward with the force of Sapphires thump.

'Thank you for the advice Sapphire. I am sure I will follow it—not!' Pearl replied. A little too curtly for Sapphires liking. Opal stood at Sapphires side giggling and blowing bubbles with a mouth filled with her favourite gum. She winked at Sapphire, all too familiar with Pearl's lack of sense of humour. Then began to take control.

'Okay, step aside, the creative one has arrived. I have a wedding to plan. I need as much help as I can get. No slacking, no falling out.' She raised her eyebrows whilst making eye contact with Pearl, Moonstone and Sapphire.

'Opal, just one thing' Queen Diamond butted in, she had been quietly standing by, and until this point was at a total loss for words, mesmerized with all the circus like activity.

'Yes, your majesty?' Opal bowed.

'Make it tasteful, not to over the top or ostentatious'

'Queen Diamond. What are you implying? All the events I plan are tasteful. I cannot believe you have the audacity to say such things, I always...'

Morganite held his hand high in the air.

'No falling out Opal remember. Especially not with your Queen. Besides, she is right. Sometimes your tastes are a little out there! Opal pouted out her lips, eyes to the heavens and started to kick her boots together in silent protest.

The crowd began to shuffle out of the courtyard towards the palace gate. It was dusk now and a curtain of pencil perfect raindrops descended from above, resting gently on their skin like the lightest autumn kiss. The perfect romantic ending to a truly emotional day for all. The Witches had not noticed how empty the palace had become. Deeply engrossed in congratulating the happy couple. Embracing each other repeatedly, smiling, and loving. Amber could not have wished for a better day and her smile was limitless, slowly consuming her face. The love in both of their hearts exuded from the light in their eyes. A couple never looked so right together. Their magical family began falling over themselves to make this wedding happen and in that very moment. They could never have imagined the devastation that would follow.

Opal took command first, forming 'the wedding committee.' Each Witch would play a part, and she insisted they must meet at 8am first thing in the morning to agree what that would be. The others were now propped against the palace walls with heavy eyes. They ambled defeated to their beds before dutifully arriving in the palace library at 8am the next morning wearing frazzled expressions. They each dragged a screeching seat around the round oak table. The chairs billowed dust out of the pink velvet cushions with the weight of each abruptly parked derriere. Morganite scowled, furiously patting the dust from the sleeve of his jacket.

'Unbelievable, ever thought about getting a cleaner!' he yelled seemingly addressing the whole palace.

'Shhh Queen Diamond is not awake yet, and that is really impolite. We are her guests!' Ruby replied crossly. Opal stood up.

'The omniscient table will select which activities we must complete for the wedding, but first I need to know the date or time?'

The Witches searched each other's faces as if looking for the answer. All returned the same vacant expression.

'Great, failed at the first hurdle. We do not even have a date or time. Where is Amber and Charles?' Opal asked, placing her elbows on the table and holding bunches of her own hair in her hands.

'Mother and Charles are walking the Palace gardens. They have so much to catch-up on. I propose we continue with the planning and select a date and time for them. They will be glad of the help.'

'Very well' Opal nodded.

'Wait a minute' Alex jumped in. 'Did you say the table decides what we do? That is preposterous!' His tone was scathing. Opal walked towards the table and placed her hands on the surface. The table lit up like a roulette wheel and began to spin. Each channeled section of the table a different colour. The other Witches drove their chairs away from the table, they were afraid it may catch their clothes or legs. The table spun, whirred and whined at a rapid pace before grinding to a slow halt. Opal gave the table a tap with a stick she had found propped against an old slate chalk board on the wall. Each channel chiseled into the table had a tiny door at the end of it which immediately propelled open. A tiny scroll of paper floated out firing into the lap of the intended recipient. Some landed with quite a force. Alex gasped as the scroll slammed into his stomach, winding him on arrival. Opal took a position close to the chalk board in ready to scribe.

'Okay, open your scrolls, read out your task and I will write it on the chalk board' she said with the voice of authority.

Alex was still struggling for breath meaning he was totally incapable of speaking first. Ruby started the ball rolling and unwrapped the first yellow parchment paper scroll. It was held together with a small fragment of string.

'Presents List'

Opal reached for the chalk and guided her delicate fingers into writing in beautiful daffodil yellow chalk on the board. She then carefully unrolled her own scroll, the paper crumbling in her clutch. Her eyes reading over each letter on the scroll. Turning on her heel she began to write. *Wedding Wear.* A mischievous smile passed over her lips as her imagination rattled wildly around her mind like an unruly child. The dress code possibilities were endless! Pearl instantly reading Opal's expression threw her back against the chair releasing a sigh of exasperation. Her arms tightly folded across her chest. She scowled at Opal with a warning glare before pushing back her own seat. She lifted her scroll which had ricochet under the table and parked against her petite slender feet. She hoped to find something on the scroll that would be a suitable blackmail tool to keep Opal firmly at bay, she feared being dressed like a doll, or worse, a circus clown. On reading her own, a smug smile radiated from her face. She threw the scroll across the table where it slid to the edge, then dropped to the floor into Opal's cowboy boot, its final resting place. Opal reached in to rescue it.

'Speeches.' Opal read aloud with a pained look of dismay. Pearl raised her eyebrows piasedly.

'Bring it on!'

Morganite carefully prized opened his scroll with tweezers not wanting to be contaminated by any dirt or dust again. It might totally ruin his outfit.

'Transport' he spat, completely unimpressed.

'Invites' shouted Alex.

'Food' Moonstone joined the chorus.

'Music' laughed Sapphire. 'And am I going to find the best tunes for the occasion!' Emerald was gazing out of the window at the garden lost in thought. Opal waved her hand across Emerald's face desperately trying to interrupt her glazed fixed stare. Emerald eventually returned from her daydream a little confused as she had lost track of the conversation completely.

'Apologies-Location, Flowers and Garden' she recited in her own aloof and distracted way.

The wedding planning was brought to a halt as the library door creaked open. Held firmly by one of the tall White Knights. Then, the familiar clicking of Queen Diamonds staff could be heard echoing across the corridors outside the library. Queen Diamond breezed in taking a moment to digest her surroundings and what she had missed.

'That makes me the Celebrant. Perfect timing!' She said raising her staff and snapping it to the floor in a decisive crack. 'You have one week to plan, and the wedding will be here in my home.' The Witches talked across each other excitedly, all cramming in extra details striving to create the wedding of their collective dreams, or so they thought. Still blissfully unaware of the nightmare it would turn out to be because somewhere in their haze of eagerness and creativity something important had been lost. Something they had not considered.

♟♟♟

The step was around two feet high and the size of a large drum kit. Ruby hesitantly stepped onto it. Opal was desperately keen to exercise her artistic dress design skills and flair at this point. She held the Opal in line with Ruby and looked straight through it. The sparks began to fly. The sparks circling Ruby and turning around and around. Then on each blink of Opals eyelids as she stared through the eye of the jewel, Rubies outfit changed. First it was trousers, then a short dress, a long dress, white, red, green, cream, purple, chiffon, tartan, fleece, cotton, silk, net, with a tiara, hair up, hair down. It was incredibly disorientating for the White Witches who watched on from ground level in absolute awe at Opals magical prowess. Ruby played the role of the model perfectly. Swinging her hips and hair with an air of confidence and pride expertly changing her expression to fit with the mood of the next outfit. The White Witches applauding her and growing increasingly excited at the prospect of each unique masterpiece. Opal may create for each one of them. Next, Pearl stepped slowly onto the platform keeping one foot off in ready for a sharp exit. Ruby gave Opal a look that said, 'do not do it.' Everyone had expected Opal to find a way to publicly ridicule Pearl. They had never been the best of friends. It was customary for any one of them to take advantage of situations which created an opportunity for point scoring against the other but to everyone's surprise, Opal always showed great restraint and professionalism. Her creativity in full flow. Carefully assigning colours and textures to match Pearls flawless, pearlescent skin and dark smoldering eyes which accentuated her every feature. Pearl remained still, drinking in the detail of each outfit, and gauging the audience approval from the expressions on their faces.

Impressed with Opals rare show of self-control, the Witches began to clap in time with the drums thudding out of the speakers buried in the whitewashed walls. It was a nice finishing feature to the palace dressing room which now had the ambience of a fashion show catwalk in Milan. Pearl glanced at her watch and leaned against the wall, lifting the weight from one leg to the other.

'Nearly there…. Okay. You can step down.'

Opal's Opal was still pressed firmly against her eye. Pearl responded by moving gracefully down the steps trying to avoid any further contact with the Opal. Moonstone suddenly let out a startled yelp. She was positioned directly behind Pearl. The others were in front and for a moment, a large thick tigers' tail had flashed into being, firmly attached to Pearl's bottom. It swished and whipped in the air. Then disappeared as quickly as it had arrived. Opal winked at Moonstone mischievously. Moonstone held her hand to her mouth and looked at the floor to suffocate and disguise her impending laughter.

Days went by before the Witches found themselves at the mockup, linen covered wedding table in the ballroom. Pearl made the finishing touches to her creation-adding a small posy of lemon flowers in the center. Flowers were Emeralds domain but, Pearl also had a hand in it, ensuring the table must mirror (as closely as possible) how it would look on Charles and Amber's actual wedding day. *Everything should be familiar to the speakers to help them to remain calm* she contemplated. Each Witch fearfully clutched their homework assigned by Pearl the evening before. Paper crumpled with scrawled handwriting serving as their aide memoires. Pearl slid a small tin can from her black highly polished handbag.

'As you will all be expected to speak on the day, this is to help with your speaking. It is a throat oil. Your voice will be smooth and clear if you use this'

She announced. She tapped each of the Witches chins impatiently as she reached them spraying into their mouths, then began striding to the next person as she continued to speak. She paused on the spot. Holding her hand on a gold-coloured pocket watch which was the size of her own dainty hand. Pearl pointed to Morganite seated on the far left of the table. Morganite let out a husky cough and Pearls long nailed, manicured finger set the pocket watch speech timer in motion.

'I can clearly recall the time I first met Amber. She was seated at the table of her mother Sylvia's table' Morganite spoke calmly and eloquently. 'I remember thinking to myself. *She really needs to do something with that wild curly hair. Her head looks like a plate of noodles*'

A roar of laughter came from the remaining Witches on the table. Pearl signaled for silence, drawing her hand across her neck in a chopping action. She extended a long finger, singling out Alex this time. Morganite pouted in objection and sat down. Alex eagerly lunged forward in his seat then said.

'Charles and I go back a long way. We are great friends. When he met Amber and told me about his feelings for her, I remember thinking. *What on earth would she want in a scruff bag like you?'* The Witches laughter filled the room. They high fived each other in celebration of their creative humour. The stopwatch clicked once more as Pearl patted Opal on the head. Opal was on her feet and straightening her creased skirt.

'I always knew Charles and Amber would end up together some day. I mean. Who else would have them?' This was too much for the group of Witches. Full belly laughs in play and rolling around the floor clutching their stomachs in the pain of laughter. Except Opal. Opal's face dropped solemnly. Her eyebrows lowering to a frown-seemingly confused by her own words. Unfolding her speech in the crumpled paper in her hand. Her eyes pass over it- reminding herself of its content. She looked to the sky as if calculating numbers in mid-air. Her eyes flickered as metaphoric pennies dropped like a sudden ambush of penny laden rain. Opals eyes sought Pearls in challenge.

'Pearl you are wicked!' Pearl flicked her hair from her shoulders in a proud victorious sweep. 'Truth serum I am guessing?' Opal asked.

'RRRRRahhhh' Pearl growled with one hand clawing the air. 'Now we are even for the childish Tigers tail stunt you pulled!'

Sapphire finally stopped laughing and drew a breath.

'I think we should all use truth serum on the actual wedding day. It will be such a blast!'

'So, it would seem. You have all already been sprayed with it' Pearl said shaking the throat oil she sprayed moments earlier.

As dusk began to fall, Alex tried to concentrate as he gazed out of the window pen poised in ready to write. The other Witches sloped off to their rooms carrying the weight of a belly full of wedding preparation. He rubbed his eyes focusing on the blank sheet of paper-waiting to be populated with wedding guest names. He had torn the paper up three times already envisaging potential disputes because of his choice of guest. He wrote Grenadine's name for the fourth time whilst scratching the lines on his forehead. *This invite might not be well received by the other guests but, I must try and focus on who Amber and Charles would like to attend. It is impossible to please all.* He reminded himself.

His fountain pen was quickly becoming dry. Hundreds of names staring up at him from the once empty sheet. This was of course literal. A magical ghost type smiling hologram shimmered above each name. It was magic! A smile spread across his face as Daylin's face lightly floated upwards from the paper. His surprise guest. This could only be good for Ruby and Daylin. The reunion might clear the air a little and it was the least he could do to reconcile the two love birds!

♟♟♟

It seemed such a short length of time before the wedding was upon them. The force field immobilized with a buzz as the guests congregated around the palace gate. The door crunched to the floor creaking and complaining with the weight of a thousand years. Hundreds of feet marching carelessly across it in an excited crowd of garbled voices now merged into a vacuum of wedding excitement. Amongst the mayhem a tall portly figure shuffled inch by inch into the palace gate. Wearing a dark grey kimono with a blood red sash.

'Hi Grenadine' a voice shouted as though they were long lost friends. The figure increased their pace, weaving in and out of the mass of bodies. A fixed and sinister look on their steely face. Eyes squinting out from underneath unkempt eyebrows. By passing familiar faces and ignoring any attempts to make conversation. They grunted heavily, forcefully thrusting their way forward whilst slowly disappearing deeper into the shadow of the palace walls.

Amber turned to face Ruby.

'What do you think?'

'Breathtaking. You look beautiful. Opal has such a gift for finding the perfect outfit!' tears brimming from her eyelids. Ruby stroked Amber's dress appreciatively diverting her mother's eyes from her tears back to the dress.

'One day, I can do the same for you' She brushed two fingers against Ruby's cheek. Amber smiled turning to the full-length ornate white mirror in her bedroom. 'Well, this is it. I cannot change how I look now!'

'Why would you want to mother? You look absolutely stunning.' Ruby gripped her mother's shoulders. She knew a hug might be too much and result in an unfortunate tangle with the wedding dress. The train of the lace embroidered dress rippled on to the floor, and the bustle at the back twisted in the direction of the train as she moved from left to right evaluating each perspective of her own profile. Ruby's lungs filled with wedding excitement as she thought of a happy ever after for her mother and in that short silence so many words were silently spoken. The room suddenly went from light to dark momentarily as a tall sinister shadow passed by their doorway unnoticed.

'Are you ready?'

'Yes, I have been ready for some time!' Ruby replied as a half-smile flickered briefly across her lips which stifled to an early death by an invasion of nerves in her delicate chest. Ruby collected the dress train-cradling it in both arms. Amber stepped carefully across the polished wooden floor then out through the doorway. Knocking on each one as she passed along the long corridor. The doors flung open one after the other as each enthusiastic guest hurriedly stumbled into the corridor to greet them. The entourage growing with every step. A red-carpet running the length of the courtyard awaited them at the foot of the stairs. The courtyard filled with unusual guests. Witches, Wizards, Dwarfs, Fairies, Owls, Dragon Flies. The list went on. Flowers spilled from each balcony in impressive waterfalls of colour designed by Emerald.

Morganite impatiently rounded up the stray guests outside the gate who had arrived late. Chastising himself out loud about the tardy arrival of some guests, as it had been the fault of his own stagecoach drivers sent from Little Love Forest. 'What happened?' he hissed discreetly at one of the drivers who was fastidiously filling his pipe with pink tobacco in ready for a well-earned break.

'Pumpkin march. Roads were filled with crazy pumpkins who wanted a pay rise' He replied casually in a farmer like accent. Morganite shook his head in disbelief.

'I have no idea what that means. I will deal with this later.' He knocked the driver's pipe to the floor to punish him and scurried away not wanting to miss the ceremony.

He returned to find Queen Diamond raised her hands in the air and the courtyard fell into silence. She turned her head to drink in the myriad of guests seated in her typically empty courtyard. Her eyes stopped at the bridesmaids. All with a distinctive and unique look of their own and in deep primary colours matching the colour of their own jewels. Her eyes transfixed by the array of colour but showing a hint of confusion at the sporadic appearance of a tiger's tail behind Pearl! Amber and Charles were now millimeters away from her gazing lovingly into each other's eyes. Charles coughed and began to stammer.

'If someone had told me this might happen, I would never have believed it. To be married to you Amber is all my dreams come true. I love you and I will make sure you never regret agreeing to be my wife'

Amber squeezed his hand reassuringly. 'I have waited for this moment for a lifetime. I love you

and I am honored to be your wife.'

'Aaaah' The guests sighed, melted by the romance of the moment.

Queen Diamond gracefully read through the ceremony and guided each word from the love-struck couple until they uttered the final words to complete the ceremony.

'Do you Charles, Eugene Clapton take Amber, Sylvia Scot to be your lawful wedded wife?'

'I do'

'Do you Amber, Sylvia Scot take Charles, Eugene Clapton to be your lawful wedded husband?'

'I do'

A hushed respectful pause filled the room as Charles extracted a tiny silver ring from his plaid green waist coat pocket and slid it on Amber's finger. His hands visibly trembling.

'I now pronounce you husband and wife'

The guests hopped to their feet clapping, laughing, crying, and embracing. A complete fusion of love and emotions. The room quietened once more on the raising of Queen Diamonds hand in the air in preparation for the final White Witch blessing. The blessing of the Diamond of Lucas Cave. Two White Knights strode slowly down the wing of the courtyard. One carrying a large gem encrusted silver box. The other banging a large drum in rhythm with their stride. Halting to the left of Queen Diamond. Queen Diamond took the box and unlocked it and carefully lifted the lid and looking into the box, the blood slowly drained from her face. Her jaw dropped in horror.

'No, no this cannot be. Where is it?'

She whispered loud enough that the crowd could hear. Her voice filled with anxiety.

'What is it your majesty?' the drum player asked. Completely puzzled by the Queens reaction.

'It is gone! The Diamond of Lucas Cave has vanished!' She screamed in an emotional outburst quite unlike the queen.

The White Knights investigated the box searching for the missing Diamond. The box was empty, and it did not matter how many times they tipped the box upside down and shook it in midair, the diamond did not reappear. The Queen desperately looked at each Knight one by one, *surely one of them would find it* she thought. The White Knights shook their heads solemnly, gesturing to their Queen, that the Diamond was not there. This was too much for Queen Diamond, all her emotions screamed inside her, she fell to the ground clutching her chest grasping at the air with her hands as if trying to catch it. All the while, her mind continually conjuring up images of the Diamond falling into the hands of the Sable Witches and how they would use it to destroy Validor and the world.

'I, I cannot breathe. The pain-' she squeaked.

'Somebody bring a stretcher!' Morganite yelled.

A team of White Knights appeared instantly with a long stretcher and collectively rolled the hyperventilating Queen onto it. When it came to the Queens health, there was no hesitation.

'Take her upstairs. I will follow!' Morganite demanded.

The guests broke into a frenzy of chatter with anyone who would listen. It was like a feeling of dread and panic fell from the sky and had infected the tone of each conversation.

'Is she still alive?' 'Who could have taken the jewel?' The guests asked in melancholic unison.

'How could this have happened?' Moonstone said, anxiously searching the other Witches faces for answers. Their faces remained grave and unchanged. They had no answers.

'I am not sure if that matters now. Queen Diamond may be very ill, and the Diamond is missing. This may have ruinous consequences for Validor and the White Witches. We are without our Queen and unprotected. Only the power of the Queen and her Diamond can keep King Organza at bay completely. Our jewels can help us against him temporarily, but his power will eventually dominate.' Emerald chipped in solemnly.

'Is there anything I can do to help?' A deep male voice said from behind. Moonstone spun around.

'Daylin, you made it!' She threw her arms around his neck with elation.

'Steady on!' He spoke. His body still swaying with the sheer force of her unharnessed affection.

'Yes. Only just made it. We had a few problems on route with angry pumpkins' he replied. Wearing an equally confused expression as Morganite had when the topic was mentioned earlier.

'Daylin … I did not know you were coming.' Ruby said her face sheepishly appearing over Moonstones shoulder she spoke quietly avoiding eye contact.

'You didn't?' He replied embarrassed.

'I thought, I thought you had asked me to come?' Ruby shook her head.

'I am afraid you were both kept in the dark. We thought it would be a nice surprise for you.' Alex interjected apologetically.

'Well, it is… Well, it was… at least until-.' Stammered Daylin.

'Yes, it is. Very much so. Just a little surprised is all.' Ruby blurted across Daylin. Trying to help brush over the awkward moment and she was ecstatic that he had joined them, and this could be seen on her face despite her clumsy attempts to hide it.

'Good. I am glad we straightened that out. Now do you think we can we get on with trying to save Validor from the Sable Witches!' Pearl said sarcastically unimpressed that they had been distracted from the Queens fall.

'In answer to your question Daylin. There is little any of us can do. Morganite will probably try to diagnose and heal. If he needs us. He will let us know.'

Her attention fell to the shell-shocked newlyweds seated at the altar. Charles held Amber tightly in his arms as she buried her head in his shoulder.

'Charles, Amber you must head back to Scotland as planned. Your powers are limited, and Charles does not have any. I am not sure you can be of any value?'

The seated guests eagerly jumped to their feet nodding in agreement and began lifting Charles and Amber from the floor.

Charles and Amber could not breathe. Now crushed in amongst the crowd of guests and being body shuffled towards Morganite's golden wedding carriage outside the gate. Amber looked back before stepping into the carriage. Her dark curls swinging with the swift movement.

'Ruby, please keep in touch. I will worry about you. I love you.' She shouted waving and blowing a kiss across the army of guests towards Ruby. Ruby reached out to catch it in the palm of her hand whilst waving with her other hand back.

21

'I love you too mother. Be sure to send my regards to the golden beetles at Lightening Pass from me!' Ruby was trying to keep things light to make the newlyweds feel a little less guilty about having to leave at such a tragic time. After all, they deserved all the happiness in the world. The carriage clattered off sparkling in the light of the burnt orange sunset.

'Have a lovely honeymoon as best you can. Please don't worry, we will take care of things here!' The guests shouted as the Carriage became a tiny spec in the distance followed by a sparkling entourage of miniscule silver fairies caught in the carriage dust trail.

CHAPTER 2

THEIVES IN THE NIGHT

Grenadine stealthy slipped unnoticed through the wedding crowd. Her heart pounding through the tightly bound black kimono. The weight of the brown leather satchel cutting into her shoulders, breathing heavily she struggled with the physical and emotional effort of the whole operation. Her black and white badger like hair glued to her scalp thick with the sweat of nervous energy. *Perhaps the Sable Witch Coven could have considered how fit she was before assigning her this task* she mused. It was probably her own fault, she as much as volunteered for the mission, it seemed like the right thing to do at the time. It had been so very crucial that she proved she was still a Sable Witch at heart and that her brief spell in Dream Cloud (a White Witch realm) had not converted her into a good Witch.

She began to recall when she first returned from Dream Cloud to the Sable Witch Coven. She had received a hostile greeting from the Dark Shadows. Steadfast in their refusal to open the gate. Their laser like eyes piercing through her soul. Scanning her for any ounce of White Witch goodness she may have been tainted with. The gateway looming in front of her-a threatening ball of fire, looming menacingly in her path, protecting the cave entrance. The fire in the gateway eventually petered out. She peered out from under her hood with pleading eyes, seeking permission to enter. One nodded its bald wrinkled head towards the gate. She crept inside like a cat, crouched low as if expecting an attack at any moment. The cave walls skimmed her shoulders leaving a thick sooty trail on her black cloak as she trod the uneven ancient cobble stones.

Icy droplets of water fell through cracks in the cave meeting her skin with a steamy hiss. A set of ancient gothic wrought iron gates were intermittently positioned on each side of the passageway. Candles smoked from aged stone ledges in the cave wall. A plague of rats scurried around, scratching the floor in a fit of madness. The walls were said to hold the worst atrocities known to Validor and the human world, that if needed, would be strategically released on the authority of King Organza as a form of attack or defense. Grenadine stayed alert. *Today is not my day to die, today is not my day to die,* she repeated entering King Organza's reception. A circular room with a blazing fire in the center. Sable Witches scattered on the stone floor around it, fur throws around their shoulders, poking dirty sticks with chestnuts into the fire, then crunching them in their mouths with their broken charcoaled coloured teeth. Their faces covered in red brand marks from the hot sticks they had fought each other with in a cruel game they relished. A booming voice sounded from a side annex.

'In here' it commanded. Following the voice, she cautiously entered a room lit by burning lanterns. She first saw King Organza sprawled across a fur lined sofa trimmed with ornate swirling antlers.

'Well, well, well' he guffawed.

'Look who it is. The traitor returns.' He held his arms out wide in a sarcastic gesture of welcome.

'I hope you are grateful. I nearly fed you to the rats. What have you to say for yourself?'

The light in the cave remained unbothered by the changing of day to night as King Organza and Grenadine composed a lengthy and elaborate plan from Grenadines' perspective. The plan was the peace offering or apology from Grenadine to the Sable Witches. In exchange, she yearned for their forgiveness and perhaps more than that, she craved high status in the Sable Witch realm more than she valued her friendship with Ruby and Amber. This was just the heinous act that could attract it.

She remembered how she burst with pride when King Organza announced the plan to the others.

There he stood loud, proud and majestic.

'My Sable Witch servants. Here me now. There is going to be a White Witch Wedding held in Queen Diamond's palace. I love a White Witch Wedding, don't you? It brings with it such, opportunity'. He sneered with one corner of his mouth lifted slightly higher than the other.

'One of our Sable Witches has received an invite, Sable Witch Grenadine'. He wafted his hand in her general direction.

'Grenadine has agreed to attend the wedding and steal the Diamond from the Crater of Lucas Cave and in so doing, will become a Sable Witch savior.' The Sable Witches cheered as King Organza gave a victorious punch high above his head. He rubbed Sable Witch Martha's head playfully who was seated close by. Then wiped his hand on her cloak to rid himself of the slime and fleas he had collected from her unkempt tousle of black crusty curls.

The Diamond from The Crater of Lucas Cave had never been in the possession of the Sable Witches. This was a Diamond which had far greater power than any other precious jewel and was superior in magic to any Sable Witch magic. How could Grenadine resist the challenge? This would be a chance to win back the favour of King Organza He had been so disappointed in her recently but in truth, if she had not befriended Ruby and Amber, she would never have received the wedding invite. She took quick sharp intakes of breath to still the fluttering feeling in her chest. The gravity of the task had connected with her breathing before bonding with her intellect.

The announcement although poignant, seemed like a foggy memory to Grenadine now. The fear in her heart still roaming without a leash as she crept away from the wedding guests. Her breathing returned to normal as she realised that she had not been challenged when she crept into Queen Diamond's chambers in the dead of the night. Passing the sleeping White Knights-who had become seemingly complacent in their duties. Grenadine had witnessed White Witch powers countless times. She did not want to underestimate their ability to thwart her plans. Only when she had successfully returned to the Sable Witch Coven with the Diamond in her possession would she feel like the mission had been successful. For a moment, she felt her heart sink with the tiny ounce of remorse for the pain she might cause Ruby and Amber, but this was soon overpowered by her entrenched thirst for King Organza's favour.

Morganite prepared the healing potion in a grey marble pestle and mortar ordered from the kitchen. His arms furiously grinding and banging the lotus seed. He feverishly sprinkled in other ingredients from small bottles selected from his tunic pocket. Queen Diamond writhed and thrashed in pain on the white regal looking four poster bed.

'Where's Pearl?'

He queried not raising his eye from the potion, pounding and crashing.

'She is on her way. She is organising the transport home for the remaining guests.' Ruby stroked Queen Diamonds head with a cool flannel trying to reduce the heat radiating from her head. Her cheeks were flushed pink, and drool trickled from the corner of her drooping mouth beads of sweat rolling down her pale forehead. 'Is she going to be okay?'

'I am sure she will' Morganite hastily replied with more enthusiasm than was real. He really had no inkling of what the Queen was suffering with. His hands trembled but he tried to disguise it so's not to create alarm. He knew deep down his magic was not strong enough to fix this but, he must try. Pearl arrived at his side drinking in the hopelessness of the scene.

'We have to summon him…. you know this' she said holding Morganite's chin in her hand and forcing him turn his head and make eye contact.

'Not yet. I need some time. I need to try.' Morganite responded-instantly, his voice trailing, dismissive of Pearls plea.

Ruby watched the conversation intently trying to make sense of it.

'Who do we need to summon. I can do it. If you think it will help?'

'Only Moonstone can summon him I am afraid' Pearl spoke loudly over the noise of the potion crushing.

'Who?' Ruby said impatiently.

'Zilante, Emperor of the Dragons' Moonstone replied from the doorway.

'We are not going there. Not yet!' Morganite pushed on. He was pouring the potion into Queen Diamond's mouth. Some of it dribbling onto the gold bed clothes. Pearl shook her head in dismay. Moonstone shrugged and held her hands in the air in agreement. Queen Diamond became still.

'Now what?' Pearl began a perplexed walk around the room.

'We wait' Morganite whispered. He slumped at the bottom of the bed. Rubbing his eyes with each hour that passed until daylight ensued.

The Queens servants' brushes bashed the skirting board as they began to clean the room. It was 7am and Ruby, Morganite and Moonstone stirred from their sleep. Morganite stood up-stretching his back. The servants opened the window to release the stale smell of sleep and potion from the Queens bedroom. The sun cast a golden path from the window onto

Queen Diamonds face. Her eyes were dazed but open. Morganite rushed over.

'Thank goodness. You look so much better!'

'No thanks to you. Things could have been much worse' A baritone voice echoed from the back of the room. Morganite visibly tensed and cringed in recognition of the voice. He turned to confirm his suspicion. A tall male dressed in a green and gold cloak towered high above them. His transparent figure floating at least two feet above ground level. His long salt and pepper coloured beard passing his feet and stroking the floor.

'Emperor Zilante' he scuffled to the floor in a respectful bow. Morganite glared at Moonstone as he did. She mouthed the words 'not my fault' and pointed to Pearl. Morganite closed his eyes disappointed by what had occurred whilst he had slept. He knew if Emperor Zilante had become aware of the day's events. There would be severe consequences for Queen Diamond. He worked so hard to protect her from this. Emperor Zilante was once the Emperor of the Dragons before his passing. His magic had been so powerful, he could return to Validor or any of his former realms, if the situation warranted it. He ruled Validor and many other realms in his lifetime. A wise, distinguished, and formidable leader-revered by most. His impenetrable midnight black and chocolate brown eyes that appeared to reach into a persons every thought.

'I am afraid I am left with no choice. I must call on the past Dragon rulers to assist me in dealing with this unfortunate and horrifying chain of events.' The Emperor said in a matter of fact but part sympathetic manner. Morganite nodded his head. Ruby, Morganite and Pearl bowed their heads. They knew better than to protest. Ruby had been awake when Moonstone summoned the Emperor narrated by Pearl. It was only now she started to feel the seriousness of the moment. The Witches stepped away from the bed as Emperor Zilante approached.

'Queen Diamond. Before I contact the past Dragon rulers. I want you to know you have been an outstanding Queen of Validor. I have watched you rule with elegance, wisdom, passion, and love. Validor could not have wished for a better White Witch Queen'. He spoke solemnly, in the knowledge that when the Past Dragon Rulers arrived, any misgivings or misappropriations during her reign would be revealed. Then, she would be judged and sentenced. Emperor Zilante had witnessed the Court of the Dragon Rulers for many years. It is a cruel and compassionless process. He wanted Queen Diamond to know that her minor mistakes during her rule must not overshadow the great ruler she had become.

'Clear the room please. Only Queen Diamond and I must remain.'

'But.' Morganite began.

'It is okay Morganite. I am ready.' The Queen croaked. Her broken voice reflecting the sadness passing through her entire being.

♟♟♟

'I do not want any part in this!' Empress Amphi implored.

Her glossy chestnut brown hair now clenched in her delicate pale fists. Tiny wisps of blond highlights straining through her grasp as if in protest.

'Please be calm Empress Amphi, your temper may disrupt the universes energy and create disaster'

The empress's handmaid's face winced tightly in ready for the response that might follow, but she knew her job was to serve the Empress. This involved keeping her emotions in check on occasion. Also, another minor concern passing through Guinevere's mind during Amphi's tantrum was that Amphi was on the brink of exploding, and if she did, she would transform from her present human image to her Dragon form and would surely burst the walls of the small tin bath!

In truth, it was a real occupational hazard. Empresses and Emperors of the Dragon Empire had magical powers far superior to that of all the White Witch and Sable Witches put together. Much worse, the young Empress had not yet learned the extent of her power and the ways it could manifest. Often resulting in one or two world disasters!

'Well maybe that is just what is required to stop this injustice. I will call it an 'act of god' again. I am sure I can get away with it!' Amphi seethed piously.

Her arms crashed into the bath water creating a wave that leapt onto the grey stone castle floor. Genevieve set to work mopping up the water with a fur lined brown towel like the exceptional handmaid she was. Water began cascading onto her apron as she did. Amphi had arisen and was now standing indignantly in the silver freestanding tub resulting in a second wave of foam topped water drenching Genevieve.

'Everything okay?'

Emperor Anthro appeared in the doorway alerted by his wife's high-pitched tone which had found its way into the castle corridor and was bouncing between the dense thick castle walls.

'You clearly have not heard the news then?' Amphi vigorously rubbed her hair with a specially laid towel at the end of the bath.

Anthro let out a breath, so long and drawn out it might have been held in his lungs for the past decade.

'No darling, why don't you enlighten me?'

Amphi whipped the towel around her slender torso. Guinevere dancing around her grabbing at the towel corners in an aborted effort to help. Amphi's face crimson and taut like she had just devoured the bitterest lemon.

'Queen Diamond has been summoned to the Court of the Past Dragon Emperors and they expect me to initiate the calling together of the court *'as is customary'*, or so they say. Totally absurd if you ask me!'

Anthro now seated on a fur clad, gold lined high back chair, exhaled a second seemingly decade old breath.

'It is not your place to fight this Amphi. I know she is our dear friend, but she has placed the whole of the White Witch realm in jeopardy by losing the Diamond from the Crater of Lucas Cave'. His one blue, one green eye desperately pleading with hers as they met.

The knot on the towel was now drawn so tight around her, her skin pinched and puckered beneath it.

'I am the Empress of the Dragon Empire. It is my place to fight if I think an injustice is in progress and one which I am expected to lead!'

Anthro waved his hand in the air as if brushing away a fly. Genevieve knew this to be the signal that the Emperor and Empress needed a little privacy. She scuttled off into the corridor making her way to the kitchen to prepare smoking goblets. Hoping this may have a calming influence at least. It was their favourite brew.

'My dear Amphi. I love you and I will support you in everything you do. You know that, but this is your duty, and you know it. Before you swore the Dragon Empire Oath of the Empress, you studied the Dragonial Laws. If a Queen of the White Witch Realm parts company with the Diamond of Lucas Cave in a deliberate or negligent manner she must abdicate. The sentence will be agreed…'

'Agreed by a committee of past Emperor and Empress peers who (although have passed into the light) will be assembled by the existing Emperor and Empress of the Dragon Empire… yes, yes, but there must be an exception. A loophole perhaps? Something that means we do not have to do this'

Amphi's towel had dropped to the floor as she needed both hands to rifle through the brittle pages of the Book of Dragonial Law which she had snatched of the shelf. Anthro rescued the towel and embraced her with it closing the book shut with one hand.

'Let it go Amphi. For better or worse. Let us do what must be done together'. He planted a gentle kiss on Amphi's soft white cheek. Then she slid down the wall, slumping to the floor in an unladylike manner. Her head propped up by her hands like it carried the weight of the pyramids of Egypt.

'Okay' she whispered

'Sorry?' Anthro questioned. He had heard what she said but could not quite believe it.

'Okay' she repeated, a decibel quieter this time.

Crystal clear tears descending her flawless complexion. Anthro drew her to her feet, passed the towel around her tiny frame. Then swept her up, cradling her tightly as they walked solemnly into the ceremonial hall. Amphi rested her head on his chest in surrender, child-like as he did.

🜲🜲🜲

The hall was silent except for the swishing of Anthro's cape as it shuffled dutifully behind him. Anthro had placed Amphi's feet lightly on the ground in ready for the audience waiting patiently for them inside.

Tapestries hung from towering walls, serving as a reminder of their position in Dragon empire history and what was expected from them. Gold framed majestic Dragon ghosts engulfed them in a powerful ensemble of paintings as they entered through the arched concrete, door less doorway. A range of prominent Dragons of historic importance. Anthro's, Wyverns – fire, gold, brost, obsidian and bone. Amphipteres and of course the dark Drakes. All beautiful and unique in nature. All colours, all shapes and sizes. Some with horns, others fur, two legs short arms, four legs but all with hard, veined wings. The paintings were accompanied by Coats of Arms posted in strategic and prominent positions in the hall each representing all the formidable clans. All equal in stature, but all with only one Emperor and Empress.

Amphi paused, head bowed close to a painting of Empress Phillipa. Former Empress of the Dragon Kingdom, an inspiration to Amphi, one of her proud descendants.

Anthro smiled warmly at Amphi, taking a further two steps towards the Anthros line. Chin held high, sharply nodding in a military way at each painting of the Anthros line-his family. At the end of the long hallway a face leapt out of a dark, well fingered painting hanging in a striking black, gold leaf frame. There was no mistaking the authoritative poise, chiselled features, and dark stone like eyes. It was Emperor Zilante. A Drake Dragon. The painting captured during his living years as Emperor of the Dragon Kingdom. This was a sobering reminder of the reason for their visit.

The Fountain of Fate loomed in front of them. A black shining marble feature, spilling liquid silver from every orifice. Anthros and Amphi joined hands tightly, gazing lovingly into each other's eyes. The room which had filled hours earlier with quietly whispering courtiers, dropped to nothingness.

Anthros and Amphi spoke in unison.

'By the powers invested in us by the Dragonion Laws. We ask our former Dragon Leaders spirits to enter this chamber. We ask that Queen Diamond also manifest in spirit form to receive her sentence. May the sentence be just and fit the crime, may our Dragon Leaders be wise and compassionate. So say we'

As is traditional. The courtiers chimed immediately after

'So say we'

The castle responded with a tremendous quake.

The courtiers began to shuffle closer to the fountain to escape its walls which were now trembling as though being ruptured by thunder. The liquid silver in the fountain began to rise into the air taking the form of each former Dragon leader.

Then with a further bubble and spurt Queen Diamond manifested. Head pointed to the floor.

The past Dragon leaders hovering, rippling and shimmering translucent, and swaying ghost like from within the fountain bowl.

'Queen Diamond' boomed a voice from the fountain.

'You are accused of negligently leaving the Diamond of Lucas Cave both unprotected and unattended. Resulting in the theft of our beloved Diamond. Do you understand the seriousness of this offence?'

'Yes, I do Dragon leaders and I am deeply sorry. I truly am' Queen Diamonds eyes still firmly transfixed on the stone floor as the tears splashed from her eyes to her feet.

'Whoever is in possession of this Diamond, now has the power to create chaos in the world of Validor and, worse, if the new owner understands its powers. They can also cause ruin in the human world. Although, we understand this was not an intentional act on your part, we have no choice but to serve the traditional punishments. How do you plead?'

'My plea is guilty wise leaders' whispered the Queen. Her legs trembled and she thought she might collapse at any moment.

'We have considered the punishments available which fit a draconian crime such as this. You could be turned into a statue and remain in the Kingdom of the Dragons, or, be turned to dust and blown from place to place as the wind dictates. However, in honour of the long and impeccable service to our beloved Validor, we the Dragon leaders think it appropriate that you are turned into a swan and spend your remaining life living on White Swan Lake'. Anthro glanced at

Amphi, he knew his wife had a hand in this, but how? Amphi gave a quick wink in reply to his puzzled expression, followed by a secretive smile.

'Thank you, wise Dragon leaders. I accept my sentence and I am grateful for your compassion' Queen Diamond sniffed in an ungracious manner trying to hold back the tears.

The Dragon leaders turned to face the fountain wall. Their work here was done. Their figures melted, disappearing into the swell of liquid silver in the fountain bowl as quickly as they had appeared.

The room gasped in unison. Amphi clasped her hands over her face and leant into her husband's chest. Anthro wrapped his arms around his wife to comfort her. Queen Diamond dropped to her knees and had she not been in spirit form, her delicate knees might have shattered on the cold hard floor. Gripping herself tightly with both arms around her tiny frame, she sobbed quietly. Amphi broke free from Anthros embrace. Spinning on her bare heels to face Queen Diamond. She rushed towards her; arms outstretched. The now loud and garbled conversations surrounding them acting as a blanket of secrecy to the conversation that took place between them.

'I am so sorry Queen Diamond. I did the best I could. I spoke with Emperor Zilante but there was very little time'. Amphi said solemnly.

Queen Diamond rose from the floor, and for the first time since her arrival, she cautiously looked up.

'It is not your fault Empress Amphi but thank you. There is one small thing you could do for me. I have only 1 hour before the spell wears off and I will meet my new life. I would dearly love to say goodbye to my family and friends before I go. I hate to ask, and I know it is against the rules. I understand if you do not want to…'

Amphi raised her hand as if to silence her. She looked over her shoulder at Anthro questioningly. Anthro dropped his head and walked away absolving himself of what might come.

Amphi dipped her hand into the silver fountain and then raised the same hand above Queen Diamonds head. Droplets of liquid silver dropped onto the Queens hologram like image. Then in a nano second, she disappeared. The guests in the room began to disperse through the stone archway back to their daily routines.

♟♟♟

'Queen Diamond, Queen Diamond!'

Morganite was gripping the Queen's shoulders shaking her vigorously. The Queen remained motionless on the floor. Moonstone and Opal joined in, shaking her arms, and gently tapping her pale white cheeks. This gave Morganite a short, well-earned break. He stood panting in the corner, leaning on the wall for support not taking his eyes away from his beloved Queen.

He gently gestured for the others to step back. He crouched down placing his head on Queen Diamond's torso. His ear pressed firmly next to her heart. His head rising and falling with the Queens every breath. Sweat dripped from Morganite's forehead. His breathing was heavy, and face flushed. The other Witches looked on. Frozen to the spot in an almost hypnotic state. Their Queen lay motionless on the floor in a strange magical slumber. Morganite stood up shaking his head in dismay. He shrugged his shoulders and walked towards the bedroom door. Moonstone and Opal following close behind. They both placed a hand on Morganite's shoulders.

'Don't leave me' a very subdued female voice said. The three Witches quickly looked back to find Queen Diamond awake and talking to them.

'My Queen' shouted Morganite euphorically. 'You came back'

The Queen started to shakily drag herself from the floor. Her legs wobbled beneath her weight almost buckling at points. With her hand outstretched to Morganite.

Morganite rushed to her side and used all his strength to pull her up. She then fell to the bed in a seated position. Back hunched over.

'I am only here for a short time my friends. I came back. I came back to say goodbye' She stammered.

'Goodbye... Where are you going' all three Witches cried out? The party like affair had quickly descended into a wake.

'I will be spending my life as a swan on White Swan Lake. It is not so bad. Please do not be sad for me. I know I can be happy there'

A mixture of expressions passed over each face in the room. It was as though they were in a relay race passing three batons of emotion named confusion, devastation, and love between each other.

'Please listen carefully my friends. I have little time left with you. You must find the Diamond before it falls into the wrong hands. You are without a Queen and unprotected. Only when you find the Diamond of Lucas Cave can you name a new Queen and protect the White Witch realm' The Queen strained to form the words with her mouth. Her hands trembling.

'I think it may be too late. I mean, the Diamond is already in the wrong hands' Moonstone said solemnly.

'How, how can you be sure?'

Moonstone closed her eyes. A rush of images circulated her head. Pictures of the events prior to the Queens sickness. She wanted to be sure of the detail, but her psychic abilities seemed weakened.

'It is with Sable Witch Grenadine and King Organza at the Sable Witch Coven. Grenadine stole the Diamond from your room during the wedding ceremony'

With that she shook her head and opened her eyes bringing herself back into the room.

'Then you are in great danger. The Sable Witches know if they can make it to the Jenolan Caves in Australia and place it on the Crucible of Doom in Devils Arch, the Diamond will inherit powers greater than all of the Dragon Emperors combined' replied Queen Diamond coughing intermittently.

'Please rest easy dear Queen. We will not allow that to happen' Ruby said earnestly. She searched the other Witches faces for reassurance but each one would not return her gaze and looked to the floor.

Queen Diamond did not notice the lack of encouragement. She grasped Ruby's hand.

'Goodbye all, Goodbye Ruby. Do not let them win. Do not let my reign mean nothing. I have made great sacrifices to look after my White Witch family. Please do not let that go to waste'

She fell to her bed from her upright position and disintegrated into nothingness.

Daylin appeared in the doorway a little sheepishly.

'I really did not mean to eavesdrop. Perhaps this is not the right time to say this but, well, I would like to help in some way. I know I do not have your powers, but I am sure I could do something?'

There was no response from the room. Each Witch shocked into silence. A silence that seemed to last an eternity until Moonstone broke it.

'Like, I know we are all feeling pretty rubbish now, but we need all the help we can get. I mean. I do not want to scare you, but the Witches are already planning something. I can feel it. Almost see it, but not quite. Maybe White Witch Sapphire could help. She can see the future.'

'She can only see the future of humans not Sable Witches' Pearl snapped in a manner which reflected her usual impatience with Moonstone.'

Opal rolled her eyes and turned away sighing.

'Okay, well, falling out with each other is not going to help the situation. We need to stay strong and work as a team on this or we have no hope' Ruby responded in a chastising manner.

'I just wish I knew what they were planning. That would at least give us a head start wouldn't it?'

CHAPTER 3

MEETING OF THE SABLE WITCH COVEN

The dark shadows stepped to one side allowing sable Witch Grenadine to pass through the cave entrance. Grenadine tried to hide the pompous smile that was smeared across her face and with her precious cargo on board, she calmly breezed through each of the corridors unobstructed. On reaching King Organza's doorway, she paused to straighten her kimono belt then wiped a clammy hand across her grubby forehead and greasy hair. *Must look my best for my big moment,* she told herself. King Organza jumped from his seat and rushed towards Grenadine greeting her with open arms.

'My dear Grenadine. How lovely that you have returned safely!' His eyes transfixed on the satchel on her back. On reaching her he immediately reached over her shoulder to open the bag.

Grenadine stepped back with lightening quick speed leaving Organza's arm grappling at thin air. Embarrassed he shoved his hands deep inside his pockets.

'Grenadine, please, sit down, my home is yours. You must be a little tired. Can I offer you some food or a drink perhaps?' Organza said with gritted teeth.

Grenadine scanned the room making sure the others around her were not also close enough to reach into her bag.

'Thank you for your hospitality King Organza. I am happy where I am thank you' She snapped back.

King Organza returned to his seat wafting an arm casually in the air.

'As you like. Tell me of your adventures then. I am extremely interested to learn of your visit to the White Witch Coven. Were you, well, successful?'

Grenadine repositioned herself. Some of the Witches had started to circle and brush against her. She could smell the stench of their skin before she even laid eyes on them.

'Yes, King Organza, I was successful. I have the Diamond of Lucas Cave'

The Sable Witches began to clap and jeer. Their raven black mud clad capes swirling and swishing, hips creaking, arms swaying in a ceremonious ritual. In stark contrast to their usual slothful demeanor.

'I, I should like to say something' stammered Grenadine.

The frivolity ensued around her. The Witches continued to dance wildly and sing. Slapping each other firmly on their backs. Spilling goblets of black spider blood wine whilst clumsily standing on each other's flea ridden wooly shoes.

'I SHOULD LIKE TO SAY SOMETHING!' She screamed trying to be heard above the chatter and merriment in the room.

King Organza stepped forward

'Silence. Our dear friend would like to talk to us' His arms waved up and down.

The room noise dropped to whispers and sniggers.

'Thank you. I just wanted to say, that as I am the new owner of the Diamond of Lucas Cave. Well, that means I could have superior powers to any Witch in this room, including King Organza. If I chose to use it. So, from this point forward. I expect you all to bow to me as your new Sable Witch Queen.'

After a pregnant pause the room broke into raucous laughter and before she could speak again, suddenly the bag was ripped from her back by a crowd of laughing Witches. King Organza lunged forward and cracked his hand across Grenadines head sending her slightly dizzy as it cracked against her skull. Her legs gave way and she crashed to the floor. Grabbing back her satchel it dropped beside her. Grenadine placed her trembling hand into it, gripping her weakened bony fingers around each point of the Diamond. The power of the diamond illuminated into action, protectively lifting her slowly into the air, her body, floating in a limp star shape. It was at that moment she felt more blows to her body. Her eyes strained to see beneath her. It was a sea of ugliness holding broom sticks who were poking and clubbing her. Her Kimono slowly becoming securely knotted in the sharp twigs of the brooms and with a final powerful yank they lured her to the putrid floor.

'Such a silly girl you are' sneered Organza.

'Once again you have tried to betray me and once again you have failed'

Grenadines head throbbed as she now lay dazed on the floor.

'Shadows, take this pathetic being to the dungeons!' Organza ordered the Dark Shadows.

They dutifully dragged the lifeless body of a rather plump Grenadine out of the room and through the dark damp corridors. She could make out a blur of endless, seemingly identical stone walls obscured by algae infested water paving the way, but to what? She could not dare to imagine. The sound of the Sable Witch celebrations still chiming in the corridors, becoming quieter and quieter with every step.

King Organza greedily rescued the Diamond from Grenadines' satchel. It was a hand sized Diamond which shone in the candlelight. Slowly its shine increased in intensity. The room now bathed in its magical glow. He clasped it tighter still, his head thrown back aloofly, his back strong and stiff. He turned cautiously in a circle displaying the jewels beauty to each Witch in the room. A multitude of eyes filled with complete awe, drinking in the magic of the Diamond.

'My Sable Witch family. Look what we have achieved. Never in our history has the Diamond of Lucas Cave been held by a Sable King. This is a momentous occasion indeed. We must not waste any time. The White Witch Coven are sure to trace this deed to us. It will not take long. Until then, we must cause as much chaos in Validor and the human world as we can cram in. WHO IS WITH ME' he concluded?

All the Witches in the room roared back to life. Clapping and chanting.

'Chaos, Chaos, Chaos'

Organza pressed his hands down to the ground as if trying to orchestrate lowering the decibels in the room.

'Very well. Sable Witches, Whitney, Redina, Yowla, Purprinkle you are my leaders of mass destruction. We will also need the Dark Shadow army, our dear spiders and a team of pixies to assist.'

Each Witch stepped forward from the masses and respectfully bowed to their King. Organza walked gracefully to a leaning bookcase propped in an alcove of the cave. He drew out a large leather-bound book and began to thumb through the crusty dry pages, clouds of dust billowed out making him cough as it hit his unprepared throat. The page turning ended, and he began clearing his throat.

'Ahhmm. 'I call upon the Diamond of Lucas Cave to assist us in our spell of Mass Destruction. Oh, hear us all mighty Diamond'

He turned the page again.

'This is the Spell of Mass Destruction'

'All that was, will not be, all that is, will be no more

Wickedness will replace kindness,

White Witches will have Sable hearts

The souls of the good will be plagued

I command Darkness at every corner and door.

Make once known paths lead to the unknown

Weaken all that is good in Validor and on earth

Let Sable Witches rule above all other, once the Diamond of Lucas Cave is placed on the Crucible of Doom in Devils Arch

My dear Diamond of Lucas Cave, make this so'

The Diamond lit up with a blinding lightening like flash. The Witches clapped their hands across their eyes to shield them from the sharp needle like light. Some yelped out loud as the light penetrated their pupils causing a stabbing, burning sensation. Organza was mesmerized by the Diamond and his glare did not waver from it. He noticed the Diamond had cracked ever so slightly down one side. Ruining its once perfect crystal beauty. It was almost symbolic of the ugliness of what was being asked of it.

Then in an instant, darkness fell it was total blackout. The Diamond or anything else for that matter was no longer visible. Lights out, candles fizzled to nothing, leaving only a path of smoke as a hint of where they once were. Silence quickly followed. Only the Dark Shadows were able to see clearly. Their bat like eyes coming to life as nature intended in the dark. It had begun. Organza spoke

'My dear Witches. This is our time to become the most powerful force in Validor and the World. Use your powers to serve me wisely. The Dark Shadows can help you find your way. Be bad, be superbly bad!'

A wave of hooves crashed onto the pebbled path as a team of black stallions came to a halt at the cave mouth. Their eyes marble white and ice cold. The Sable Witch transportation had arrived. The Witches now wrestled each other, grabbing at their horses, and clambering on. Their charcoal black cloaks and horses merging with the darkness of the night. Screeching and chanting as they cantered to meet their wickedness. Organza leading the charge from the front, on their path to absolute chaos. A swarm of flies following closely behind as their uninvited entourage, following a trail of sewer like odors.

Whitney bravely moved to the front of the crowd, close to the hooves of King Organza's horse.

'Your Majesty' she panted

'I am honored to be part of the mission, but do you have a plan, I mean, where are we going?'

Organza glanced back, trying to remain focused on the direction of travel whilst answering Whitney's question.

'Yes Whitney, first we pass through Pixie Land. We need a little back up from our dear friends. Then onwards to Lightning Pass, tell the others, final destination... THE Crucible of Doom in Devils Arch'

'Where is that my King?'

'The Jenolan Caves, Australia!'

Whitney nodded.

'As you wish' She replied pulling the rein upwards as she turned to face the other Witches. She shocked in her seat a little before she regained composure. A shock of white ice coloured fog travelled across the group, swirling around their wicked heads. 'First destination Pixie Land, then Lightning Pass comrades' the fog whispered magically into their rotten ears.

'Hurrahhhhhhh' the Witches let out a loud battle cry in unison.

♣♣♣

Forging ahead through the wall of darkness, the stallions galloped tirelessly. Fueled by a dangerous concoction of magic and hysteria. Hours passed, and more blackness, then more blackness ensued. Yowla passed a gnarled aged hand in front of her face to see if she could see it but it was impossible. Nothing was visible. The stallions drove on relentless and regardless. Their eyes, although unsettling on appearance acted as powerful searchlights. Yowla took deep breaths. This was a completely unsettling experience even for a Sable Witch. A new unfamiliar world, where everything was invisible but not. A complete loss of their visual senses. Whitney stroked the silken main of her horse. Trusting this Devil's animal to carry them safely to Pixie Land. Trust in the Devil, a total absurdity, but at this very moment it was paramount to her survival.

After it felt like almost a lifetime had passed, a sea of voices floated towards the group. Shouting, moaning, cursing, crying and they could see. Tiny lights flickering over Pixie Land, flashing, and weaving like sparks from a fire. Pixie Land gate barely visible from fifty yards but the sound was loud. Beyond the gate, whistling sparks travelled across the sky and glitter floated in the breeze as if a glitter pillow fight were in motion. It appeared that the Pixies and Fairies were at war!

'Take that pesky Fairies! hit them with the glow sticks guys' shouted a long-nosed Pixie. He held a stick taller than himself, striking the air around him. The Fairies skillfully steered around each stroke. They danced a beautifully choreographed dance high above the Pixies head making a real mockery of their inadequate attempts to hurt them. The whistling shrined through the air. It seemed to be coming from the direction of the Fairy Queen, two fingers jammed under her tongue navigating the fairies with the other hand into areas of safety.

'What fun!' Cackled King Organza. A rancid grin spreading ear to ear.

'It's a Fairy v Pixies battle' Whitney murmured quietly. 'What do we do your Majesty?'

'We needn't do anything Whitney, just watch the entertainment' he delighted.

Organza waved creating a barrier with his arms, gesturing to the other Witches to stand back. The stallions slowly stepped away from the Pixie gate. Close enough to see, but far enough away not to be involved.

Suddenly, the Pixies doubled in number, popping out of their homes in the ground at an alarming rate. The fairies flew in a frenzy, bending and stretching, ducking and diving to avoid the impact of the glow sticks. The younger Fairies cracked to the ground with the impact of the glow stick blows. Their eyes rolling around in stupefied confusion.

'YES, YES!!' Organza mused. 'WHAT FUN, GO THE PIXIES!'

The shrill of the Fairy Queen whistle sounded again. Each Fairy glanced at the Fairy Queen as soon as it was safe to do so. The youngsters lying on the floor now writing in the pain as the Pixies used them as a steppingstone to the next unsuspecting victim. Straining their eyes in the direction of their Queen. She leaned forward, tapping a red Pixie gently on the shoulder.

'Ahhhhmmmm' The Pixie looked up in response and as quick as a flash, the Queen grabbed the glow stick from the Pixies hand and bashed him on the head. The Pixies legs thrashed and wiggled beneath him, before he passed out. He flopped limply to the floor. The Queen glided down smashing the top of a Pixie house which had started to emerge beneath her. The house popped like a balloon. She smacked another as hard as her delicate arms would allow. It popped like a balloon full of goo. The Fairies did not need a repeat demonstration. They grabbed at the glow sticks imitating their esteemed Queens example and with each rise of a new Pixie house a series of popping balloon sounds followed as the Fairies pierced each one by one. It was like a giant amusement arcade game. The younger Pixies who had survived the massacre hauled themselves to their feet, but they lacked the strength to pull the glow sticks from the Pixies. The Fairies were growing in strength, now having most of the glow sticks in their possession. The Queen knew she must help the younger Fairies. She reached into the thoughts of the Pixies talking telepathically and loudly inside their minds. 'STOP HURTING THE FAIRIES OR YOU WILL MEET YOUR DEMISE, STOP HURTING THE FAIRIES OR YOU WILL MEET YOUR DEMISE' she shrieked at a voice level that no human could withstand without causing substantial ear drum damage. The Pixies clasped their ears to rid themselves of the Queen's voice in their heads. They stumbled around unable to place one foot in front of the other. Allowing the smaller Fairies to steal a glow stick and submit meaningful blows to the back of the Pixies head.

King Organza looked to the sky in embarrassment and steered his stallion around to face the Witches to his rear.

'I have seen enough; what a pathetic display, it is clear the Pixies are not strong enough to help us. Let us leave them too it and push on'

'Perhaps we could assist the odd little creatures. I would not mind splatting a few dainty yucky Fairies' Yowla sneered.

'Not necessary, Yowla, it would be a waste of energy which we need to preserve. It is wiser to pick our battles. If a bunch of teeny tiny Fairies can overpower the Pixies, they are of no value to us'

'As you wish your majesty' sighed Yowla.

'ONWARDS to THUNDER TUNNEL AND LIGHTENING PASS!' Commanded King Organza.

The horses brayed back into action, hooves clattering on the stones with the noise of a thousand castanets.

CHAPTER 4

THE PLAN

"What happened here? Did somebody die?' Alexandrite whispered into Daylin's ear. Instantaneously reading the silence and solemnness on each Witches face as he cautiously enters the Queens bed chamber.

'Queen Diamond is no longer with us. She has been sent to White Swan Lake to live as a Swan' replied Daylin trying to bring Alex up to speed without causing any more suffering to the others in the room.

Alex scratched his head, screwed his face up revealing the lines of a life of many smiles.

'How, I mean, I don't get it. She is the best Queen Validor has ever known?'

'I know right?' Daylin eyes were still wide with disbelief from the whole recent chain of events.

'Well, well we cannot just stand here expecting the Diamond to come to us. I am headed to Lightning Pass with or without you' Daylin said, trying to stir everyone into action.

The Witches stood motionless. It was like he had not spoken. Moonstone quietly sobbing into the ruffles on her dress.

Pearls fingers smoothed the wisps of her raven black hair into a position of faultless perfection.

'Wait, if we are going to do this, we will do it in a coordinated fashion. This requires a formal meeting of the Coven'

The Witches understood what this meant and fell in line, before shuffling out of the room towards the library, engulfed in a cloud of black silence. The library door protested as it opened for the millionth time since time began, moaning as it let a blast of dusty air into the pristine corridors of the palace. The chair legs magically bending their legs whilst stepping away from the table in ready for the Witches to sit in their usual positions. Once seated, Pearl spoke first.

'If we want to find the Diamond, this will take all the magic we can muster and even then, it may not be enough. We must all prepare to go through Lightening Pass'

Daylin paced the room for the millionth time.

'Well as I said before, I am in?' His jawline snapped into place, set and firm.

The other Witches eyes remained fixed on the walls in a trance-like state.

'Someone needs to stay at the palace. I know the Sable Witches are not here, but the Pixies are?' Emerald whispered.

'Very well' Pearl nodded.

'You will remain here and guard the palace'

'That must be you Emerald.' Pearl replied.

Emeralds eyes quickly began searching the others faces, *why always her* she mused. Her gaze was met by a vacuum of silence a tell-tale sign that she was firmly in the frame for the job. She reluctantly rose from her chair nodding to each Witch respectfully, then disappeared through the door. Daylin paced faster this time, his athletic legs striding and springing in each direction. The sound of his breath could be heard above his footsteps now. He clutched the chair of each Witch one after the other and leaned close to their ear. First Morganite, then Pearl, until he had spoken with each one in turn.

'Come on, dig deep, for the sake of Queen Diamond. Say you are with me, please?' he repeated.

Ruby turned and looked into his green pleading eyes, still as deep and clear as the purest lagoon. She remembered them all too well and her heart began to melt.

'Ruby, I know you are grieving but I need your help. I cannot do this alone?' he continued.

Morganite coached out a tense strained sentence and rising from his chair next to Ruby he gripped Daylin's muscular shoulder.

'We are all with you Daylin. We are feeling a little shocked is all. Give us time'

He circled the room with his stare as he spoke. Letting a large sigh emerge from his plump lips.

'Let us all take this evening at least to collect our thoughts. Then at eight am sharp tomorrow morning we meet at the palace gate. Is that okay folks?'

The Witches stood once more, still muted by their grief, they quietly dispersed into the hallway.

Pearl and Daylin remained in the room. Daylin slumped into Morganite's still slightly warm chair. His trowel like hands dropping to his thighs. Slapping his skin with a thwack as they came to rest.

'We need to agree how we will get to Lightening Pass. Then what the next steps are once we get there, and I am not sure where to start'

Pearl responded by standing up and beginning to sketch a plan on the wall with a single glowing fingernail. Daylin joined in on occasion interjecting with new ideas, and together, they worked through into the early hours of the morning. A cockerel began to crow somewhere in the distance as a firm reminder that daylight should have been upon them, but they were still surrounded by the deathly blackness of the night sky wrapped around their every part. The blackout had not shifted, and their brief time to mourn the loss of their beloved Queen had passed. It was now time for action.

The Witches jumped up from their beds on hearing the thud of Emeralds fist on the thick mahogany sleeping chambers door.

'Get up, get up, no time to lose!' Her deep voice ricochet across the halls of the castle.

Moonstones kicked away the pink silk covers. Her leg flopping to the floor adorned by the grubby thousand-year-old pink striped wooly sock her mother knitted for her when she was five. Her hair standing high on her head as if she had been electrified.

'What. what on earth is going on. Emerald, is all that shouting necessary at this time in the morning?'

Moonstones legs had now become fully entwined with the cover during all the commotion. She slid to the floor and began crawling to the door, the cover locked onto her leg was coming along for the ride. Alexandrite tripped over her blanket as he also raced to attention into the corridor. Then Pearl, complete with eye mask took flight over the complicated bundle of Alex, Moonstone and the bed clothes and in one giant lump the tried to desperately wrestle themselves free. Opal leant on the doorframe; her body bent double with laughter at the whole scene. Unable to resist a chance to be creative. Opal swirled her hands in the air as though directing an orchestra and the blanket seemed to follow her hands, it was being charmed like a snake. Alex, Pearl and Moonstone had no escape. The cover had become part of them almost and was fixed to all their legs.

Ruby had joined the circus late and was looking on, scratching her head. Then Morganite emerged gracefully into the crazy corridor antics.

'Guys, guys. What on earth is going on? Do you realise the seriousness of the situation? Stop wasting your magic on silly tricks!' Morganite yelled.

Opal's arms folded across her chest and her lips pouted.

'It was not a silly trick; it was duvet art' She protested giving a quick reverse magical twirl of her fingers to untangle them all.

Ruby scooped up the blanket and launched it back into the chamber in the hope this would remove any urges to carry on the corridor comedy sketch.

'Okay, we should head downstairs and to the castle gates. There is much work to do' she said in an authoritative manner.

Opal shuffled behind, this time using her magic to switch the Witch's clothes to save them some time. The Witches strode on oblivious to the fact that they were now dressed like ancient Japanese warriors. Their heavy leather skirts and boots cracking loudly with each step. All eyes focused on reaching the castle gate. Helmets perched proudly on their heads. It was a powerful sight. Time was of the essence. The gate whined open with the shrill squeaking sound of metal on metal. The group close together in a protective huddle in the darkness. Their breath making mist in the night air. Pearl pushed through to the center of the group. Her teeth chattering in her attempt to speak.

'Whilst you were sleeping, Daylin and I plotted the map we will travel.'

'Sister, I hope you are not suggesting we walk to Lightening Pass. I thought we would travel by the light?' Grumbled Sapphire

'That would mean we would be seen in the darkness surely?' Ruby interrupted.

Daylin smiled. 'Yes Ruby, you are correct, and as I am human, that would exclude me from the plan and Sapphire, don't worry we will not be walking'

Ruby blushed at the half-implied compliment from Daylin.

'This is how we will travel' he said, pushing his fingers deep into his mouth he then let out a piercing whistle. Just for a moment Ruby was sure she saw fire spark from his lips. She rubbed her eyes and looked again. The whistle continued and the other Witches clapped their hands over their ears. The spark like fire had disappeared as if it never existed. As if it had not been dark enough, suddenly the whites of their eyes disappeared as if it never existed. Now everything was completely invisible. Moonstone passed her own hand across her face to check if it was still there. Then clumsily slapped herself across the face.

'Oooow, that hurty!'

'You okay?' Ruby checked and before Moonstone answered, suddenly, the floor in front of them was alight in a path of flames. The girls recoiled in fear, trying to work out where the fire had come from. They traced it path a far as it went and could not believe what they found at the end of it and at the end. It was a Dragon!

'This is Nodrog, please don't panic'. Daylin shouted above the crackle of the fire.

'He is friendly. He used to live with Charles in Little Love Forest. My Father also lives there and is now taking care of him'.

'Awesome' Moonstone yelled slapping the scale like giant torso of Nodrog. Nodrog opened his friendly eyes wider, in a Dragon type smile.

'Hi Nodrog' they chanted in unison.

Once Rubies fear had subsided, she gently stroked his head. Nodrog looked up child-like, then nestled his head into her delicate hand. Pearl took charge.

'We must travel in twos. Nodrog will taxi each of us to Lightening Pass, more than two of us would be too much for him. We will travel over Pixie Land, pass the Stream of Undying Love, Over Little Love Forest and onto Hope Coast. Lightening Pass is just along the coast side'

'Any questions?' Pearl looked across the group. Her tiny body quivering with the cold.

A voice was heard 'I am afraid of heights'

Pearl spun on her heal, trying to locate the voice.

'Who said that?' She asked sharply.

'Me....Sapphire' was the reply in a far less blithe voice than the Witches were accustomed to from Sapphire.

Daylin gently touched Sapphires forearm.

'You can come with me. I will hold onto you' Sapphire gave an unconvinced smile. Not the least reassured that this would help but she had come this far and did not want to let anyone down.

'Okay, here are your couples' started Pearl

'Daylin and Sapphire, Ruby and Opal, Myself and Alexandrite. That leaves Moonstone and Morganite. We will travel to Lightening Pass as couples. When we reach the other side, we must find our way to the Jenolan Caves in Australia. This is where the Crucible of Doom in Devils Arch is and ...'

'Stop, wait, what on earth are you talking about. This is starting to feel like a bad horror movie' Sapphire panted, beads of sweat flowing from her forehead and trickling down her cheeks. She leant against Nodrog to steady herself.

'If you would let me finish Sapphire' Pearl snapped back.

'The Sable Witches need to take the Diamond of Lucas Cave to the Crucible of Doom in Devils Arch and place it on it. If they are successful. Well ... it does not bare thinking about'

Ruby was the first to speak after a short, confused silence.

'What would happen? I think I need to know.'

Moonstone blew a chewing gum bubble before saying.

'Bye Bye world and the Sable Witches have enough power to rule any empire, including Validor' She pressed her fingers to her temple like a gun to emphasise the point.

'Boom, Boom – I only know because the Jenolan Caves are back home. We are brought up knowing about this stuff.'

Pearl screwed up her eyes in a chastising stare.

'Thank you for scaring everyone Opal'

Opal took a sweeping bow. Holding her helmet at the same time.

'Always a pleasure honey'

Pearl jabbed Daylin in the back.

'Okay, let us get on with it. You go first'

Daylin gave a cold unruffled stare.

'In a moment Pearl. I think we need to say our goodbyes first'

Alexandrite placed an arm around Pearls pale shivering shoulder. Pearl knocked it away as though an annoying fly had come to rest upon it.

Nodrog spread his large green veined wings and began to furiously fan them as if warming up for a marathon. This threw gusts of wind in the direction of the Witches. The noise and momentum was akin to being stood too close to helicopter blades at takeoff.

The Witches wobbled on the wind. Their feet shuffling in every direction the gale dictated. Daylin gripped Rubies arm to steady her. He tried to speak but the strong wind suffocated any sound that tried to find its way through it. He looked at Ruby's unusual battle armor and was a little baffled. Ruby looked in the direction of his gaze and shook her head in disbelief. Pointing to Opal and shrugging her shoulders. This was sign language to Daylin that Opal was behind their usual attire.

Daylin cupped Ruby's ear and spoke into it.

'I know this must seem kind of scary to you, especially as you will be the first to leave, but always know that I will protect you. Please trust that?'

Ruby looked to the floor, hiding the tears that had begun to brim from her eyes. Daylin placed his other hand under her chin and lifted her face towards his and their eyes met.

'Alright, break this up guys. We are all freezing, and if I do not get on the Dragon soon, I might change my mind!' Sapphire interrupted. Ruby and Daylin jumped to attention in unison. Daylin grabbed Ruby and began to push her front first up Nodrog's torso. Ruby seemed to master the climbing of his wiry scales like an expert. Opal was in short succession. Scrambling in a less lady like fashion from scale to scale rather athletically. Ruby and Opal looked below them at the other Witches who now seemed like tiny miniatures.

'Bye all of you' waved Ruby.

'WE WILL BE TOGETHER SOON IN MUCH BETTER CIRCUMSTANCES. I FEEL SURE!' she shouted.

Opal bumped up next to her and grabbed her by her tiny waist. One hand steadying herself on Nodrog's spikey spine, the other gripping Ruby. For half a second she let go and made a thumbs up. Mouthing the words in Daylin's direction

'I got this. I will make sure I take care of her'

Daylin returned the thumbs up with a pained expression. Not utterly convinced. He knew Opal could be a little wild at the best of times. He patted Nodrog gently on the head. Nodrog licked his hand with a long wet black forked tongue.

Then scrambled to his feet which had been hunched beneath him to shorten the climbing distance for the girls. They swayed a little with the sudden movement, but managed to stay in position. It was like riding a camel only fifty times larger.

Nodrog took a large step forward, his wings still flapping with great force, then he began to run a thunderous sounding run across the cobbled footpath. Then with a last swoop, they had launched high above the others. The Witches strained to see them high above their heads, but they had quickly disappeared. Cloaked by the black velvet daytime sky. Followed by silence.

'Do you think they are okay?' Moonstone asked biting her nails.

'They will be okay. Nodrog will keep them safe' Daylin answered reassuringly as he gripped her shoulder.

'Well how long do we wait, I mean, it is cold' Pearl trembled.

Alexandrite began to chant under his breath. It was not clear what he was muttering. It was almost like a foreign language but within nano seconds balls of fire leapt from the palms of his hands and onto a pile of old wood sitting in the next field. The Witches did not need an invitation. They ran in the direction of the fire as quickly as their heavy armor would allow. They quickly formed a circle around it, huddled together for warmth, patiently awaiting Nodrog's return.

'We could always wait inside?' Pearl protested.

Daylin shook his head firmly.

'No, it is no longer safe in the castle. We would be too vulnerable, and I want to be sure I do not miss Nodrog on his return'

Pearl slumped to the floor. Arms tightly folded across her chest. Eyebrows dropped low.

Hours and hours passed and one by one the Witches lay down next to the warm crackling fire and started to doze. Daylin remained on his feet he was never off guard duty.

Emerald had never felt quite so alone. The others left hours ago, and she was unsure where they were or how they were doing. The castle was eerily quiet. The only way she could find out would be to message in the sky with her Emerald or contact them psychically. She tried to reach Pearl for a short time using her psychic ability, but there was something about the daytime darkness that was acting as a blocker to her entering Pearls thoughts. Emerald decided the only thing she could do was to contact Amber who would be in Scotland by now. The darkness would not have spread further than Validor at this stage, she felt sure.

Are you there Amber, Ruby is on her way to earth with Opal? I am afraid there has been a terrible chain of events. Queen Diamond has been sent to White Swan Lake to live the rest of her life as a swan. The Diamond of Lucas Cave is missing, and the Sable Witches have it. Validor is in darkness. The others have left the White Witch Coven to try and find the diamond. Are you and Charles safe?

She spoke the words in her head clasping the Emerald for comfort.

I am here Emerald. Charles is asleep. It was a long journey home. I cannot believe this has happened and I feel I should have stayed to help. Is there anything I can do?

Emerald closed her eyes in thanks

Thank goodness you are okay. It is not your fault. The only thing you can do is keep a watch for the others and help them if they pass your way. Stay alert and safe please!

CHAPTER 5

ON A DRAGON'S BACK

Ruby's stomach churned at the memory of a thousand turbulent bumps in the air. It did not help that she had missed breakfast this morning. She could just make out Opal in front of her, she was stretched out on the grass; hands propped behind her head. A short grass stick protruding from her brilliant white teeth. Nodrog had propped himself against a Willow tree and was stroking pieces of debris from his wings. They looked like strange shadows in the dark.

'I could eat the world' Opal plucked another blade of grass from the ground and placed it in her dry mouth.

'Me too, if I remember correctly, once we enter Lightening Pass the Golden Beetles will provide us with something to eat' Ruby replied.

The entrance to Lightening Pass was now only a few footsteps away. It flickered brightly almost glowing through the blackness. Nodrog's large lumpy chin rested on the grass. His eye lids dropping and lifting as he fought sleep. The Smoke still billowing out of his nostrils which could be heard and smelled but not seen. Opal set herself in motion dusting remnants of the floor from her hands.

'Well in that case, let's not wait any longer. Let's do this!'

Ruby began to push herself with both hands off the floor. Her arms were weak and giving way a little under her own weight sending her stumbling to attention. Opal hooked her arm through Ruby's. They looked each other in the eye, nodded in a business-like manner and turned to face the entrance. Ruby bent down and passed her tiny hand over Nodrog's monstrous bottom in a grateful stroke.

'Thank you Nodrog. Stay safe on your travels. I hope to see you soon'.

Nodrog lay motionless his body rising and falling with each smoky breath. Fast asleep with exhaustion.

The closer the Witches came to the entrance, the more powerful its magnetic draw was. There was no turning back. Soon they found themselves dragged into the tunnel. Their bodies floating weightlessly in the air. Ruby could see Opal slightly ahead of her. She remembered the last time she was here, the Beetles dressing her and feeding her. Such beautiful gentle creatures but this time the tunnel seemed so dark and unwelcoming. *I hope they arrive soon* she thought

♗♗♗

Nodrog awake from his half sleep. His giant jaw yawning almost sucking in the willow trees limp branches as he did. His big blue eyes shining and alert, surrounded by long brown fluffy eyelashes. He began to lift his wings once more. Raising then dropping them. Raising then dropping. After a few warmup stretches he made his way back to his friends. His wings creaked and cracked at first. Then they sprung back into life as if remembering what their master was asking of them. One massive, clawed foot stepping ahead of the other as he gained speed in ready for take-off. Flapping vigorously, he tried to gain height. His body slowly rising from the floor, now almost ten feet in the air. Then there was an almighty crash. His left wing had met a tree branch. He swerved towards the ground, dropping at quite a pace, until thud. Nodrog raised his dazed head, checking for any damage to his wings. He was stunned but not deterred. Once again, he began the usual ritual to propel himself into flight. This time rising more effortlessly. Finally, he was on his way.

Daylin was seated next to the fire now. He had started to feel a chill. Pearl clambered to her feet. She placed one hand on Daylin's back and gave it a light pat. She stood in the exact space Daylin had occupied minutes earlier. It was almost like they had swapped guard duty and it was second shift. The others lay motionless with only the crackling sound of the fire to be heard. The stillness did not last. Suddenly, a cloud of wind swirled around the fire which had reduced to nothing more than sticks of glowing orange embers. The Witches armor started to tremble against it. It howled around their ears swooshing with all its might. The Witches sat bolt upright one after the other in something resembling a chorus line. Scrunching their eyes at each piece of stray dirt which tried to find its way into them. Daylin was the first to hop to his feet, one leg still dead from sitting on the hard ground.

'Ladies, I know that sound. He said excitedly. He is coming back. It is Nodrog, he is coming back!'

The Witches were standing now, and they raced over to Daylin, and stared into the distance in the hope of seeing a glimpse of Nodrog. The sound growing with every second until there was nothing. The wind faded away and they were once more in total darkness.

'False alarm I guess' Pearl scoffed.

Daylin carefully placed his hand on her mouth to quieten her.

'Shhhhh, wait for it! He pointed again to the sky.

A skidding sound could be heard coming from the trees. It grew louder and louder. Closer and closer.

'Stand back!' Daylin shouted. Waving his arms to direct the Witches behind him. Moonstone was unresponsive. Still slightly dazed from her broken sleep.

Then BANG, Moonstone was catapulted into the air.

'Aaaaaahhh' she screamed before falling to the ground in a huddle of bones.

The others swung around totally confused by the whole chain of events before they were greeted by those giant big blue eyes and a familiar teethy smile. It was Nodrog. He was back!

Morganite rushed to Moonstone and began to feel her arms and legs, almost like a doctor examining his patient. Except instead of medicine, he added a touch of soothing magic. Moonstone smiled as the blood started to flush back into her pale shocked cheeks.

'That was a rush. Thank you Morganite!' Moonstone gushed.

Daylin laughed and stroked Nodrog. He had never been so pleased to see him.

'My friend, welcome back, we were getting a little worried, I must admit, but I never doubted you!'

Nodrog's tongue suckered Daylin's face leaving it shining with wet drool. The Witches erupted with laughter. Daylin gave a tired wide smile as he rubbed the slobber from his cheek.

'Okay, Moonstone and Morganite, climb on' directed Daylin. He patted Nodrog's back as he spoke.

Moonstone shuffled slowly towards Nodrog at a snail's pace, still a little bruised from his grand entrance. Morganite placed two hands on Moonstones back carefully propelling her forward. Moonstone winced and swept his hands away smoothing her leather skirt like armor as though mentally preparing herself for what might come next, she eventually reached Nodrog. Swallowing loudly, she took a deep breath and began to scale his back. Gripping pointy scale after pointy scale, clambering to the top of what felt like Mount Everest until she finally reached his prickly spine. On doing so, she threw one leg over to the other side of his back, almost overstepping as she did. Nodrog gave a gentle wriggle straightening her up into a safe position. Morganite puffed and panted as he heaved his bulky six-foot frame, tracing the path Moonstone had taken only seconds earlier. Then with a blink of the eye they had disappeared into the deep velvet black sky.

Moonstone tilted forward to avoid the gust of wind which had sent sand into her now streaming eyes. Her face pressed firmly down on Nodrog's back, she squeezed her eyes tightly shut, clenching her teeth at every flap of Nodrog's wings. Mile after mile they flew through the never-ending sea of black soot sky.

Daylin, Alexandrite, Sapphire and Pearl had been playing 'name the ballroom dance' for hours. The woodland mice being the unwilling participating dancers, powered by a spot of harmless magic of course! Adjourning ballet tutus, the mice strutted the fox trot and the waltz totally disenchanted by the whole experience. The campfire still burning at low ember throughout. Pearl yawned and clapped simultaneously breaking the spell the mice had fell victim of, leaving them to scuttle away, grumbling unreservedly as they did. They had become accustomed to the Witches using them for entertainment and it was never a pleasant experience. Once they reached the foot of the forest, they turned to face the Witches boxing the air and sticking out their tongues in retaliation to their earlier treatment. They lacked the courage to do it too close to the Witches as they feared they may become fire roasted toast!

Nodrog had returned once again and was sitting patiently next to the fire. He seemed puzzled by the scurry of mice into the woodland and sometimes struck out a clawed clumsy foot in an unsuccessful attempt to play with one. Alexandrite cupped both hands together in a cradle. He signaled with his head for Pearl to step onto it. Pearl walked gracefully over and placed a tiny foot into his strong hands. Then propelled herself up Nodrog's calm resting torso. Alexandrite not too far behind, was watching carefully and paternally for any potential slip or fall by Pearl which may require an act of rescue on his part. They both made it without effort to the top. Grinning from ear to ear they high fived each other. Hands upstretched to the heaven they crashed them together, ending the victory gesture with a squeeze of each other's hand which remained clasped for a little longer than had been necessary. Looking adoringly into each other's eyes. Daylin coughed loudly not wanting to interrupt the moment.

'Okay, nearly there now. I am not far behind you. We need to stay focused on the Diamond or none of us have a future right?'

Pearl looked down sheepishly in the realisation that Daylin may have witnessed the romantic feelings she had for Alexandrite. The same feelings which had followed her since being a child which had always been her secret, for the most part. Alexandrite placed both hands around her shapely waist to secure her in seat. Pearl knocked away his hands, resisting any further surprise shows of emotion. Alex was unperturbed and unbeknown to Pearl, lightly gripped the leather straps on her armored skirt. *I am not losing you, whether you like it or not* he thought. They launched into the air and began their long journey. It felt like an age before they were on the ground and facing the entrance of Lightening Pass. Both captivated by its glowing beauty. Alex made his way over to it.

'Are you ready?'

There was no reply. Pearl had not moved and was some distance behind him. Petrified, her feet seemed to be unwittingly glued to the spot. Alex looked around.

'Pearl?' He reached his long arm out towards her.

'Take my hand, I won't let you go. I am not going without you'

Pearl took a tentative step forward, then froze again, shaking her head from side vigorously.

'I don't want to. Something just doesn't feel right' She squeaked.

'It is okay to be scared, but I am with you. Please trust me. Come on. You and me against the world?'

Pearl began to walk towards him. Her legs shaking with each step. She was soon at his side. Alex gripped her face with both hands.

'Have I ever let you down?' He questioned.

Pearl shook her head. Alex dropped his hand and reached for hers.

'After three, one, two....three'

They both leapt into the tunnel together, feet first.

Daylin blew and puffed. His hand clasped ungentlemanly like to Sapphires generously sized behind. She had slid back down Nodrog's back three times now. Daylin wrestled her uphill once more. He was quickly running out of energy.

'Do you think you can move your hand from my butt?' She yelled leaning down to face him.

'Sapphire, this is the only way. We have tried every other. Can you please try to pull yourself up with your hands? I will push from down here'

He shouted back, the trails of her armored skirt scraping across his face as he spoke. He winced in pain.

'Alright, alright, I am trying my best!' she panted.

Even Nodrog looked to be raising his eyebrows in despair. They both lay across his back at the top gasping for air. Eventually regaining their composure. They swung one leg over his scaly spine and thrust themselves upright into flight position. Nodrog quickly rose into action, following a kind pat from Daylin who had become increasingly concerned that they might never get there.

'Whoa, oh no, I don't think I can do it. Get me off!' Sapphire complained.

'Hold on tight and please calm down. Shut your eyes if it helps. It will soon be over' answered Daylin.

♟♟♟

Grenadines' knees hurt. Her legs had been crouched close to Lightening Pass entrance for too many hours. She had forged ahead of the others, desiring to impress King Organza and had successfully arrived hours earlier. The pound of hooves descended on her ears. Their deafening crescendo clattering ever closer. The shine on King Organza's long golden tresses glistening in the dimness as they surfed on the breeze. Grenadine found this unsettling for a Witch of his origin. *Far too clean* she pondered. On the cruel yank of each rein by the hard-hearted Sable Witches, the army of horses slowed to a standstill at the mouth of Lightening Pass.

Grenadine greeted them with arms open wide and an ugly beaming grin.

'Your Majesty, I am glad you arrived safely. May I say how magnificent your hair looks and …'

King Organza raised his hand dismissively

'Yes, Yes. Enough of the groveling Grenadine. What have we missed?'

The others cackled at Organza's absolute disregard for Grenadines' compliments.

Grenadine contemplated not telling them all in retaliation. She bit her lip for half a second before blurting out all that she knew. Her behavior like that of a child desperately needing her Father's attention, but always failing to receive it.

'Your Majesty, I have seen most of the Witches pass through Thunder Pass. Well, all but Daylin and Sapphire but I suspect they are on their way!'

King Organza raised an interested eyebrow.

'You mean, through Lightening Pass child, they passed through Lightening Pass?' He stared at his nails awaiting the answer.

'No, Majesty. They travelled through Thunder Pass. I switched the tunnels before they arrived!'

The others gasped. Then looked away not wanting to show Grenadine how impressed they might be with her cunning wickedness. King Organza gave a wry smile.

'You have done well Grenadine. Very inventive indeed, what horrors they will face!'

White Witches are forbidden to travel Thunder Pass and Sable Witches cannot take Lightening Pass. The consequences of taking the opposite path are said to be catastrophic. All Witches were warned of this from an incredibly young age. However, Organza began to drop the fake smile that had been on his face moments earlier and began to stare a look of a thousand daggers in the direction of Grenadine. He placed a long, sharp, elegantly painted fingernail on the tip of Grenadines' nose causing her to wince.

'You forgot one small thing. We can only direct Thunder Pass to one place per day. So, before I left the Coven, I directed the pass to Australia and there it will stay, for the next twenty-four hours!'

Grenadine leant forward as if waiting for the punch line. She had no understanding of the meaning of Organza's words.

'In other words, you just sent all the White Witches to Australia. Nice work, they are now ahead of us?

He smashed his hand across Grenadine's head knocking her sideways on her feet.

Yowla fought to the front of the group, her own horse butting heads with each of the other horses as she did. The others wearing a dazed expression with each bump.

'Let me help. There are other horrid things we can do. First, the shadows will make it difficult to pass through the tunnel. They may not make it and, what if Daylin and Sapphire never get here? That would be even more fun?' She jeered.

Grenadine pouted. Not wanting to be outshone.

'Let us send the Bats!' They all cried their eyelids flickering rapidly with the thought of the horrendous battle that might be.

The Witches shrieked in excitement. Organza had already began waving his wand in midair, painting shocks of silver light with each ignition of its magic. Every swipe resulting in a new bat receiving their instructions and coordinates, taking them directly to an unsuspecting Nodrog, Sapphire and Daylin.

Yowla rushed forward to the front of the group.

'I could use some potion to stop Ruby and Opal?'

Another excited cheer came from the Witches. The evil energy surrounding them reaching an all-time high.

King Organza closed, allowing his wand to drop to his hip. His eyes now heavy with the travel and the evil magic he had conjured.

'Our work is complete; we must now pass-through Thunder Pass ourselves. It is time to take the Diamond of Lucas Cave to its rightful place. The Crucible of Doom in Devils Arch. Follow me'

The Witches dismounted their horses whipping them into action with stick like crooked wands, sending them scurrying into the surrounding dense forest shadows. They then raced each other on foot, into the entrance of Thunder Pass screaming like a family of starved hyenas.

♟♟♟

The sound of Sapphires moaning had started to grate a little on Daylin.

'Try to imagine you are in a place where you feel safe. That might help?' Daylin hollered. His voice in battle with the sound of the wind whistling around their ears. He offered reassurance and comfort as best he could, but nothing seemed to pacify her. Daylin squinted down at what should have been the floor. Hoping to see some sign of life or at least an indication that they were close to Lightening Pass. As he did, Sapphire let out a shrill scream. In the momentary second that Daylin had looked away, Sapphire had lost her balance and was sliding at great speed down Nodrog's back. Daylin tried to grab her ankle as she passed him by, but it was too far to reach and soon he was distracted by a sharp blow to his head. The pain was excruciating. He gripped his head with one hand and felt blood starting to drip from the base of his head. He knew something had hit him *but what.* He could see nothing but the black of the night. He strained his eyes looking deep into it, trying to penetrate its walls. It was then he saw something, a tiny speck of deep red tiny light, then another and another. Daylin gulped, fear and anger bubbling up inside him. He was only human, and nothing could save him from what he knew was to follow. He was surrounded by Vampire Bats. They were ducking and weaving around them, patiently waiting for their opening and moment to bite. There was no mistaking them, their familiar black thick sinewed wings covered in the devils fur and laser like red eyes. He could barely hear Sapphire now but suspected the bats had been instrumental to her fall. His heart sank to the bottom of his feet. Total despair filling every void in his being. He began to think the worst. *He might never see Ruby again, or his Father.* He trembled as the combination of terror, sadness and the ice-cold night seemed to invade his bones. The bats now in their thousands, swarming around both his own and Nodrog's head. Nodrog has started to crash his wings harder, smashing those bats beneath them to smithereens. He threw his head around to glance at Daylin and when he saw Daylin covered in blood, his eyes filled with sadness and large marble like tears began to descend his emerald green solid cheek bone. He opened his massive jaw, revealing his spindle like pointed teeth. Then let out a wail. The sound was like the song of a tribe of beached seals. Daylin's fingers hurt as he gripped Nodrog's spiky spine even more tightly now, his ears ringing with the sound of Nodrog's cry. He did not understand Nodrog's intentions until he saw something strange in front of him. Perhaps his eyes deceived him. *Am I in heaven or hallucinating?* He cogitated. A hundred Dragons had appeared in the night sky. All colours of the rainbow, all shapes, and sizes. Ducking and diving between the gaggle of bats and with each flap of their wings sending the powerless bats clattering to the ground. A bright yellow Dragon was on his left, grinning ear to ear.

'Hi, my name is Bessie. Master, take her hand and pull her over?'

Daylin looked puzzled at the fact that the Dragon was speaking, but also that he didn't really understand what she was asking.

'You can speak. Dragons can't speak. At least that is what I heard?'

'Some can speak to some people, not all. No time to explain now. Pull her over' The Dragon replied still beaming. Daylin came to his senses when he realized what she was trying to say. Sapphire was perched upright on Bessie's back. Her hair a mass of wind crushed curls and her eyes saucer like with horror. Daylin reached out and dragged her to his side with all his strength. A sudden surge of energy and adrenaline rushing through his veins. Sapphire managed to pull herself upright and was now seated as close as she could get to Daylin. She clutched her chest desperately trying to catch her breath. Bessie gave that all familiar white gleaming smile and disappeared into the crowd of Dragon wings. Sapphire straightened her body armor scowling as she did. Her hand moved to her neck and she began caressing her Sapphire. The power of the Sapphire took over, the tension visibly lifting from her face in an instant. She then gently stood up, confidently and with the grace of a ballerina. Her feet arching and gripping Nodrog's spine like a tightrope walker to a rope. Daylin knocked away the bats attaching themselves to his suit. His mouth gapped open as he witnessed Sapphire standing tall on Nodrog's back. Even the draft of hundreds of flapping wings did not sway her. Nodrog and Daylin carried on, still desperately clonking every bat they met, sending them crashing to the ground. Sapphire lifted the Sapphire from around her neck and gripped it tightly in her palm. Then raising it high above her head began to chant the words

'Peace, Vrede, Peace Vrede, Peace, VREDE!'

On the last holler of her final word. The bats and the Dragons stopped fighting. Instead, they floated around one another as though they were completely oblivious of each other's existence. Their once clumsy sharp wings now floating lighter than air in the dense black sky. Sapphire pressed her jewel the Sapphire against her forehead and it suddenly blazed into light, making a perfectly straight path for miles across the sky. The bats and Dragons coasted to the light, almost hypnotized or seduced by the light as they began to merge with it. Now soaring high above and farther and farther away from Nodrog and his White Witch family. The sound of calamity and battle following closely behind them. Only the gentle comforting flap of Nodrog's wings could be heard. Sapphire gave a childlike jump into the air, then landed with a thud in her original seated position on Nodrog's back. Daylin began pushing his jaw left to right with his hand, wincing as he did. The first attack from the bats had really left its mark.

'Wow, Sapphire… I mean…you saved us!'

Sapphire gave a deep belly laugh which seemed to go on for minutes. A total release of tension that had been built throughout the attack they had endured moments earlier. Daylin placed his thick arms loosely around her neck in a friendly embrace.

'Thank you, Sapphire, my heroine!' She gave out a loud deep chortle once more. A laugh that said, I am so glad this is all over.

'You are most welcome my friend' She stroked his arm before he released it to regain his grip on Nodrog's spine whilst noticing a small trace of blood on his hand. She twisted around and scanned Daylin's face. There were drops of blood running down the left side of his cheek. She turned back to face Nodrog.

'Nodrog, we need to land. We need to check Daylin's face before we go any further. Do you think we can do that?'

Nodrog gave a slow bow of his heavy head in a nod and began to descend. After a short flight, they could make out the shape of trees and a forest below them. Then they were down, they seemed to be in a clearing of some description. There was a heavy scent of flowers in the air. Daylin drew a deep breath and began to sniff loudly.

'I know this scent; it smells like lavender. I think we are in Little Love Forest. Sapphire, we have landed in my hometown!'

Sapphire looked around, and sure enough a carpet of purple lavender covered the floor all around them.

'Great work Nodrog. Okay, over to you Daylin, lead the way!' Sapphire smiled making a courtesy gesture with her arm.

Daylin began to walk down the familiar cobbled path adjacent to the Stream of Undying Love which led across the village. The lanterns were in plain sight now decorating the path with their orange flames, licking their way out of their boxed captivity. Most things were as he remembered. Except there were no people. *Where were the people?* At this time of year, the path would be strewn with lovers and 'want to be' lovers all making their wishes, close to the Stream of Undying Love. Instead, there was an unsettling nothing and nobody. Although he found this disturbing, he did not mention the change to Sapphire. She seemed more relaxed since they had landed, and he did not want to make her anxious. They began to walk along the path and had walked for around ten minutes, giving Nodrog a break from his usual flying taxi duties. He plodded alongside them, leaning to chew the plush green grass on occasion. If he gained any distance on his friends, he would pause and roll in the grass until they caught up. It was on his third pause of this type he felt a poke. He raised his head to find himself nose to nose with someone. A worn lived-in male face peered into his football sized eye, one pressed firmly to his lips. As if to say 'silence' Nodrog gave a bewildered smile and nuzzled into the fresh grass. Suddenly, the man leapt down in front of Daylin and Sapphire landing in a muddled huddle at their feet. Once he had regained his composure, he lifted a now dazed heavy head and spoke.

'Surprise' in a voice half the volume it should have been. His head dropped back to the floor at rest as if the word surprise had exhausted every ounce of his energy.

'Father?' Daylin whispered.

'Father, is that you?' He began cradling the man's face in his great big hands.

'Yes, Daylin, I wanted to surprise you. I guess I am too old for the acrobatics huh?'

They both laughed the same family laugh, only one a little lighter than the other, Daylin's a little younger in sound. Their arms wrapped around each other in an intense, long overdue hug.

Sapphire waited until their embrace was at its end and offered her hand.

'Hello Daylin's Dad, I am Sapphire'

'My apologies, Sapphire, this is my Father Duke, Father this is Sapphire a White Witch from Validor and one of my good friends'

They loosely shook hands, like strangers do, accompanied by a polite nod of the head.

'Forgive me', Duke said apologetically.

'Come along, I have a warm fire and a glass of wine waiting. Oh, and a gumball for Nodrog of course'

Nodrog heard the word gumball and sauntered over to join them, planting a big wet slurp of his tongue across Dukes cheek. The grass instantly losing its former appeal. Gumballs being his favourite sweet which Professor Clapton (Charles) had made part of Nodrog's staple diet. They trudged onward through the quiet woodland with only the sound of their footsteps for company.

'Father, where is everyone. What happened?' Daylin asked.

'Well son, when the blackout came, some people left the village as fast as they were able. Others are still locked in their houses, only venturing out for food. All of them are so afraid of the Sable Witches arriving. No magic to save our people I am afraid' Duke replied matter-of-factly, followed by a wink in Sapphires direction.

'So long as the Sable Witches have the Diamond from the Crater of Lucas Cave, there is no magic to save anyone' Sapphire shrugged.

They soon arrived at the tiny wood cutters cabin where Duke and Daylin lived. The door creaked open and, as promised, the fire blazed in the corner. The dark wood walls and matching furniture making a homely and welcoming scene. Daylin sat down on the tired green ripped sofa. Duke patted the seat next to Daylin.

'Please, do sit down Sapphire. Make yourself at home. I will find something to bathe that cut on your head Daylin!' Duke delighted.

The clock on the wall chimed 7pm. The travel had consumed the whole day and, if night were not already permanently with them, it would now be dusk.

'If you do not mind, I really need to get some sleep. I am exhausted and I guess you guys have much to catch-up on?' Sapphire yawned.

Duke jumped to attention. Then pushed open the oval wood paneled door closest to him.

'Of course, please have my room. I can sleep on the sofa.'

He allowed her to pass under his arm.

'Thank you Duke, and Goodnight' Sapphire gave a half smile with the only small drop of energy she had left. Duke nodded, then closed the door lightly behind her. Duke returned to Daylin on the sofa and set about cleaning the rather nasty cut on his head. The blood had now become quite a horrid decoration on Daylin's face. Red, dry and sticky trails plotted paths across his face and had dried brown in the wind. Duke used cotton buds to clear it, gently dabbing until there was no trace of blood except that which was still visible in the cut itself. It was a labour of love and a task he was more than happy to do for his son.

'Do you want to tell me what happened?' He asked

'Bats Father, we were attacked by a plague of bats. I honestly thought we were not going to live, but then Nodrog made this strange sound and Dragons appeared from nowhere. They got us through. It was a miracle. I still cannot quite comprehend what happened!'

Duke leant forward and stroked Nodrog's head. The only part of him that could join them in the tiny house. His head crammed through the window almost occupying all the front room. Duke pressed his fingers together deep in thought. He pulled himself up from the chair and walked towards the tall oak dresser behind the sofa. Reaching into the draw he retrieved a dusty old oval framed photograph frame and rubbing the dust away with his hand, he passed it to Daylin.

'It is no miracle Daylin. It is your family' he said his voice cracking with nerves and emotion. He had wanted to tell Daylin about his ancestors for so very long but could not find the right moment.

Daylin took the frame and stared at the scene. It was in black and white, but the images were still clear. He could see a picture of a woman dressed in regal clothes. Wearing a fur lined robe and tall crown. Next to her was Duke wearing the proudest smile he had every witnessed. In the background were two Dragons. They were Dragons but very different in appearance than the others he had seen before. The smaller one had two legs and two arms like claws almost fastened to its wings. Clearly female. The other was bulkier and greater in height. A male it would seem, with four legs.

'Do you recognize the lady in the picture?' Duke searched Daylin's face for a spark of recognition. After a momentary pause, he saw what he was looking for.

'Is that mother…It looks like mother? Why is she dressed that way?'

Daylin leaned closer to get a better look at her features.

'Yes, it is your mother or Empress Wyveen as she was known for a short time in the Dragon Empire. This was our wedding day. The Dragons behind her are her Mother and Father. Emperor Zilante and Empress Winifred. On a Dragon's wedding day, Dragons change from the human form to their Dragon form. They hold this form throughout the ceremony, as a mark of respect to their ancestors'

Daylin's eyes grew wide with fear and confusion. He didn't speak for some time. Drinking in what he was hearing but not quite believing it. His mind cascaded back to a time when his mother was alive. He pictured her wearing simple rag like clothes with a head scarf tied around her head, trailing dark curls peeping through it as she helped Dad chop wood for the villagers in the garden.

'I do not understand. We are human. We have no royal heritage or magic. What are you saying Father?'

Duke took the picture from Daylin and rubbed his hand across his mouth. His lips trembling as he fought against the sadness rising in his chest.

'Your mother should have been an Empress of the Dragon Empire. When the child of an Emperor and Empress marries, the Emperor and Empresses are expected to pass on their throne to the newlyweds. Except, your mother fell in love with a simple wood cutter. So, she could never be an Empress if she married me'

He began to sob uncontrollably into his hands. The guilt oozing from every part of his being. He had always believed that Wyveen would still be with them if she had not lost her Empress Powers and become human. On the night she died, a Sable Witch had thrown a fireball threw the village. All the houses slowly burning away. Families crying in the streets as they watched everything, they owned turn to a cinder. Wyveen had bravely fought through the smoke, dragging family after family into the safety of the street. When she found herself at the last house in the village. Once again, she walked through the flamed entrance to rescue the last family. Never ever to return, because that night, she lost her life. Duke was often distraught in the knowledge that had she still been a Dragon Empress, she would have walked through that fire unscathed. This is a burden he had carried for so long. He never really understood how her family could disown her just because she fell in love with a lowly human, but they raised Daylin as best they could. Daylin was only ten when he lost his mother, and he knew how his mother had died. His Father often spoke of her braveness and selflessness. The beautiful virtues she carried deep inside her, which eventually led to her death. That inner beauty, combined with a Dragon like lack of fear for fire (which had never left her, despite the life she chose for herself). Daylin placed an arm around his Father's shoulder. It had been hard for them both, but they had always had each other and the memory of an amazing mother and wife.

'Father, why didn't the Dragons help mother the way they helped me last night?'

Duke recovered himself and began to speak once more.

'Although the Dragon rulers abandoned your mother. They made a promise to her, that her children would not be abandoned, and later in life, if her children married another member of the Dragon Empire, they would still become Empress or Emperor of the Dragon Empire.

This means you will always be protected by the Dragon empire and one day, if you marry the right person, you will be Emperor and Empress of the Dragon Empire'.

Daylin sat speechless in his chair. He looked from the photograph to his Father, then back to the photograph several times. Drinking in this whole crazy notion that he could one day be a Dragon Emperor

'But why would I want to be part of an Empire which treated my mother so badly?'

Duke nodded and squeezed Daylin's hand.

'Your mother wanted this. She made the Dragon rulers promise that if she could not rule, her children should not also be punished for her choices'

Duke reached into his shabby checked waist coat pocket and took out a heavy gold pocket watch. He never took the waist coat off, and it had become battered over the years with every blow of his wood cutting axe. He forced his fingernail into the clip and the catch released. Then passed it to Daylin. Daylin peered into the watch cover to see a ring. The ring had a large triangle shaped Diamond sitting proud on the rings cradle.

'Your mother's engagement ring. It is yours now'

He closed the watch cover and dropped the watch and chain into Daylin's hand, then Duke closed Daylin's fingers tightly around it.

'Please treasure it and when the time comes, give it to the person you want to marry'

Daylin met his Father's pleading stare and returned it with one of love, adoration, and sincerity.

'Thank you, Father. I will. Do not worry. It is safe with me'

Duke rose out of his chair. A little punch drunk with the roller coaster of emotions but relieved that the secret was out. It had been a load on his mind and a big responsibility to pass on his wife's wishes. Daylin stood alongside him and gave him a manly thump on the back, followed by another heartfelt embrace. Daylin shuffled an energy less walk into his long-missed bedroom. It was time to rest before he was on the road once-more.

CHAPTER 6

SHADOWS AND
EARTHQUAKES

Ruby's heart was racing around her rib cage as if trying to make its escape. Her ears filled with the screams of a thousand deaths. The walls around her dripping with green slime, plopping into puddles of goop on the tunnel floor. *What is happening, this is not the Lightening Pass I remember?* She panicked.

Opal was a tiny dot in the distance, floating further and further away. Ruby circled her arms in a front stroke. Trying to swim through the air to catch Opal. Her frantic arm motion sending her closer to the floor and the goo beneath. One foot had become firmly set in it now. Ruby thrashed her ankle from side to side with all her might, finally releasing it from its sticky prison. Her shoe was not so lucky. It was firmly jammed in the goo. Ruby looked back, there was no possibility of reaching it now. She didn't need the shoe as much as she needed her life. Her body was totally at the mercy of whatever evil magic was present in the tunnel. She hurtled through the tunnel. The little wrestle with the gunk monster had its rewards, it had tossed her frontward now at a tremendous pace and she could now see Opals athletic figure now within arm's reach.

'OPAL, WHAT ON EARTH IS GOING ON!!' she bellowed

'WE ARE IN THUNDER PASS, THIS IS NOT LIGHTENING PASS, KEEP IT TOGETHER, AND THIS WILL BE A MONSTER RIDE!' Opal laughed, always happiest in the face of a challenge

Ruby took a large gulp.

'Okay' she croaked. Her head in a total spin, locking her gaze intermittently on every strange, shaped shadow rippling on the walls. The tunnel was filled with the sound of howling wolves which penetrated their heads, soon becoming the only thing they could hear. Black arms grabbed and tore their clothes, reaching out from the walls. Each tear cutting into their soft skin. Opal fervently wrenched Ruby away from the shadow like arms each time she became trapped, and Ruby returning the favour for Opal. The putrid stench of sewers all around them. They both gasped for breath, battling their way through, and fighting off every outstretched arm emanating from the tunnel walls. Ruby was now pinned to the filthy walls, several arms wrapped tightly around her torso, she fought for breath and began to wriggle in protest but was unable to escape their deathly tight grip. Her eyes began to close as she slipped into unconsciousness, her lungs now completely starved of oxygen. Opal swam through the air with every drop of energy in her veins. Pushing herself forward, getting closer and closer to Ruby with each wave of her slender arms. Opal reached into her armor and clutched her Opal. She closed her eyes tightly and murmured.

'Be creative, rarrk, rarrk, be creative' her heart shaped lips pressed against the Opal.

In the blink of an eye, the arms became still and were frozen to the wall. Ruby slid away from them as they began to reposition themselves flatly against the wall. Opal seized Ruby's hand and began to pull her through the tunnel. The shadows had formed quite a unique pattern on the walls. So perfectly arranged, it was almost like wallpaper.

'Very creative!' Ruby winked.

'Some of my best work!' Laughed Opal showing a perfectly formed row of big white teeth. As they continued their strange swimming dance. It was not very long before they saw a crack of light at what looked like the end of the tunnel. A welcoming but intense beam of light. *Nearly there* they both thought. They each leant their heads to one side so that they could meet. Leaning on one another in a comforting way, and there they stayed as they crept the final inches to the end of the passageway. Ruby's mane of dark hair lightly intertwined with Opals short spiky blond crimps.

The horses were dotted around the unsightly gaggle of wicked Sable Witches, stepping around in that drunken stagger horses do, almost as though the ground is too hot to stand in one place for any length of time. Perhaps their hooves had tired from the marathon journey across Validor and through Thunder Pass. The Sable Witches all wore matching scowling expressions, the sunlight making them wince in a pained squint. They were seemingly unimpressed at the opposite climate conditions they had met since departing Validor. This was not the bleak darkness they so enjoyed. This was in stark contrast, and they were never enamoured with the cherry glow the suns ray inflicted on their haggard skin. All except King Organza, the vainest of the group. He was of pale, young complexion. A carefully nurtured porcelain type face created from the best fairy blowtox potions Validor coin could buy of course! He did appreciate a sun kissed look from time to time, and this was one of those times. This Sable Witch Coven stood close by; their heads covered by the all familiar Sable Witch black capes. Blood red hair snaking out from one of the hoods, the trademark tresses of Witch Redina, always a giveaway of who she was every time. Similarly, Whitney's paper white strands, Yowla's yellow sickly custard-coloured curls and Purprinkle's shocks of deep violet hair served to betray their disguises. Not forgetting Grenadines Skunk like stripes.

'Okay, gather around. It is time to raise some hell!' King Organza beckoned to the others, waving his arms inwards towards his own chest.

The others did not need to be asked twice. They created a tight circle. Lifted their hands into the air, splaying their fingers apart. Their little fingers hooked together linking the evil group together. King Organza sucked in a breath of air, then released a stream of grey smoke which meandered into the middle of the group, swelling in size as it did.

'Choose your weapons, my lovelies, let us use our magic to resurrect the Sable Witch Legends of Validor' he invited Yowla into the middle of the circle with a sweeping hand gesture. Yowla began to speak loudly.

'I choose Armando the Werewolf to be the companion of Morganite and Moonstone' she sneered a yellow toothed, crooked smile. Then stepped back out of the circle. As the words left her lips, the smoke began to form the shape of a giant Werewolf, complete with long pointed ears, needle like claws and a swirling long tail.

Redina shuffled forward next.

'I choose Astro the Troll to be the companion of Alex and Pearl' This time the figure of a round short male with a long nose, dropping ears and a short grey beard could be made out in the smoke. The werewolf type figure had now disappeared into the sky above. The dwarf took the same path.

'I call the Ghosts of the Ice Valley three sisters to be Ruby and Opals new friend!' shrieked Whitney with a cursing proud crow.

King Organza clapped three times. The smoke split into three parts, this time creating three silver shimmering shapely female figures.

Purprinkle was last. Grenadine did not understand the ceremony, so she watched quietly, drinking in all the wickedness.

'I choose the Merciless Mummy, to be the companion of Emerald' she exclaimed.

King Organza pushed an appreciative bony finger into Purprinkle's shoulder as the Mummy shape floated high above them.

'Well done Purprinkle, I had almost forgot our little Palace guard Emerald. The White Witches do not stand a chance'

The Witches jumped up and down, bouncing excitedly, sometimes stepping on each other's feet out of sheer devilment.

'Wait, Wait!' Grenadine shouted, raising her voice a decibel higher than the victory chorus.

'Hate to burst your bubble, but what about Daylin and Sapphire?'

King Organza raised his hand in the 'silence' gesture they all knew and loved. The noise level dropped to nothing.

'Good call Grenadine. I will invite my friend Dotty the Monster of Lucas Lake to take care of those two' he continued. This time dusting his hands in the air as drops of dust formed the shape of something vaguely resembling a tyrannosaurus rex before taking flight.

♣♣♣

It was a beautiful forest. A sea of lush green uniformed trees standing tall around them, bowing and stretching in 'tree like' yoga positions against the force of the wind. Astro began to tap his arms and legs. As if checking he was all in one piece. Armando looked on, then started to mimic Astro Not quite certain why they were doing it, but Armando was not the brightest of werewolves and was renowned for his copycat ways. The three sisters whispered away, giggling, and pointing in the direction of Astro and Armando. The Mummy sat up stiffly on the floor, in tightly bound dirty white bandages. Astro propped his hands on his hips in a superman gesture. This only accentuated the little protruding pot belly he had acquired over the years. The girls giggled even louder.

'Okay, okay, what is so funny?' He said as he glanced crossly, casting his angry eyes across each of the girls faces. The sound of the girl's voices, eerie and unsettling. Their voices echoing in a ghost like manner, each time they made a sound. Their words rebounding of the trees so that it become impossible to decipher where the voices originated, they seemed to come from all directions. Their mouths remained tight shut throughout, as if they were not speaking at all. Astro covered his ears. It sounded like a badly made horror movie. Armando also placed his hands on his hips in the superman pose and pushed out his tummy. Glancing at Astro to compare and measure tummy sizes. He needed to confirm he had

98

pushed out his tummy sufficiently enough to match Astros. He then repeated

'Okay, okay, what is so funny?' in an identical voice to Astro. Then covered his ears in just the same way to copy his newfound friend.

Astro jumped on the spot. His face flushed red, and eyebrows dropped into a stern stare.

'And you can stop it too. What is this? Am I the source of everyone's entertainment?'

'Not mine, I do not find you remotely interesting. Can we get on with this? Does anyone have any idea where to find the White Witches?' Mummy started to power himself up off the floor with both arms, as much as his tight outfit would allow. Armando placed his head on Astro's shoulder batting his eyelashes and grinning. Astro immediately pushed him away as he started to feel Armando's wet slobber drip down onto his neck.

'Great, so once again the Sable Witches have assembled us, and we have no clue how to fulfil their wishes!' Astro puffed. Armando puffed too making the same perplexed grimace as he did. Astro slapped Armando across the head making a loud 'Thwack' sound. The three sisters let out a concert of raucous ghostly laughter.

'We know' the three sisters echoed in unison. They held out their hands revealing three glass like baubles. Inside were images of the White Witches, each in quite different locations.

'Ruby and Opal are in Scotland with Ruby's mother. Daylin and Sapphire are in Oberon Australia. Morganite and Moonstone are here in the Blue Mountains and Pearl and Alex are in Freshwater in Sydney' they all chanted in Chorus.

Astro and Armando crept closer and peered into the shimmering light of the baubles. The Mummy hobbling closely behind. The scenes were transparently clear, it was as though they were watching a tiny film inside the balls. Each scene in the film showing each White Witch and what they are doing right now. Morganite and Moonstone were traipsing some never-ending concrete steps. Heavily shaded steps that seemed to stretch to the heavens. Daylin and Sapphire trudging alongside a river in Oberon. Sapphire was chatting and collecting beautiful purple flowers. Ruby and Opal were seated at Amber's fireplace sipping a cup of hot chocolate and Pearl and Alex laying in a quiet cove next to the sea with the waves frothing and crashing at their feet.

'Well, it seems the crazy chorus line of ghosts have some uses after all!' Astro clapped.

'If you call us that once more, we will not help you. You need us, so, be nice' They said in a taunting voice. The girls were now holding hands and skipping in a circle as they spoke, or didn't speak, at least, not with their mouths. Their white lace dresses dancing around their legs with them. The Mummy cleared his throat.

'Okay, ladies, you made your point. I also need to find Emerald. So, how do we do it?' he leaned heavily forward, then back as if correcting a crick in his stiffened back. Armando started to do the same until. 'Thwack' Astro interjected with a crack of his hand across Armando's head once again. Armando crashed to the floor this time, his eyes wide and bewildered. The girls stopped dancing and gave Astro a warning stare.

'For you Mummy, it is easy. You need to find your way back to Thunder Pass. It will lead you back to Validor. For Armando, he is already where he needs to be. Astro is a little more difficult. You have a way to go. You must find your way on foot to Freshwater. We could provide transfer, but we don't like you' Once again, they executed their haunting dance, holding each other's hands once more, as they broke into wicked laughter, they were completely oblivious to Astro's pleas for help. He tried to tug at their ghost hands, desperate to get their attention. Instead, he slipped through their transparent form, falling face down on the ground in the middle of their circle of sisterly love. Armando steadfast in his mimicking activities dove to the ground next to him. Standing, then diving again, just to make sure he performed the dive just as Astro had.

'I have had enough of this circus. We are supposed to be scary legends of Validor not the Pointer Sisters or circus clowns. I am out of here'

Mummy stomped away; eyes transfixed to the ground. It was clear he was attempting to create the maximum distance he could from the group and at the greatest possible speed.

♆♆♆

'What a blast that was, thought I had almost lost you for a moment' Opal jested, giving Ruby a masculine pat on the back. Ruby sat at the mouth of Thunder Pass, desperately trying to catch her breath. She could feel the warmth of the air bringing her frozen hands back to life. She starred into the dazzling sun light, drinking her old friend in. It had been a long time since they had spent any time together. The balmy heat began to gently thaw her tiny icy cold body. Opal flopped down beside her flapping her arms and legs wide apart, as if surrendering to the heat. She clawed at her head armour, carefully dragging it from her sweaty, hair clad helmet. Her hand reached into her pocket and produced her namesake Opal. She placed it against her eye, just as she had done at the wedding practice and directed it to Ruby and then herself. In a flash, they had both changed outfits. Opal back to her trademark white denim shorts, white cowboy boots and white

Stetson and Ruby in a beautiful white summer dress which made her look like a fairy. Ruby stroked the fabric.

'Thank you Opal. Very appropriate!' She gave a grateful smile and began to fuss with the creases forming in her crisp white skirt. Opal nodded and gave a straight smile. It was so still, and extremely quiet. A little breeze passed over them. So very peaceful. Opal closed her eyes, and it was not long until Ruby felt her own eyelids start to drop. They lay face to face without a care in the world.

The tree branch creaked as Yowla began to shuffle to its farthest point. She gripped it with both hands trying to silence it. Slowly she leaned a wiry arm forward so that she was directly in line with the two girls below her. Opal and Ruby shuffled a little. Trying to find a comfortable position on the hard ground. Yowla released a dash of yellow powder from her palm, and it started to whirl through the air in the direction of Ruby. She watched, as it dropped lightly to the ground next to Ruby who was still sleeping like a baby. Yowla gave a silent victory punch in the air, then reverse shuffled back up the still seemingly protesting tree branch.

'I think we need to get up' slurred a weary Ruby.

'Really, I was just starting to sleep?' Opal pouted.

'Yes, I think if we just go to the left a little, we may find some signposts or something?'

Opal was already standing and forcibly dusting the soil from her hands. She began to walk in the direction Ruby had pointed too, Ruby only a footstep behind. Then, suddenly and without warning, there was a loud creaking sound. The girls looked to the ground in the direction of the noise. A huge crack had appeared underneath their feet. Ruby gripped Opals hand so hard her knuckles shone white. Her eyes wide with horror. The sound of the earth cracking beneath them was deafening.

Opal tried to hold onto Ruby as the crack between them grew wider and wider. Ruby looked down at her feet before a further crack caused her to wobble and loose her footing. One hand still firmly holding onto Opals. Opal leaned into the crater, squeezing Rubies fingers with all her might. The pain was excruciating, she did not know how long she could hold on.

'Don't let me go' Ruby croaked

'I am trying to hold you, but your hand is slipping'

Opal's hand was slipping away from hers, the mix of sweat and dust making it impossible to hold on. She was now left with nothing but fingertips, until she grasped at thin air. She was gone. Opal could see her plummeting into the cavernous black hole faster than the speed of light. Opal leapt to her feet, quickly wrenching her cowboy boots off. She took five long strides back, then squatting down like a sprinter, she ran like a whippet towards the mouth of the crater. On reaching, it she launched herself in headfirst. Her heart pounding in her ribcage whilst the gravity pushed it somewhere close to her throat. *What am I doing* she thought? Possessed by a deep-seated desire to save Ruby. She fell and fell, for miles it seemed, travelling so fast she had no concept of how far. She heard a cry from beneath her.

'Grab the grass!' It spoke. She took a moment to realise It was Ruby's voice, and no sooner had she heard it, she was passing her like a runaway train. In that split second, she saw Ruby hanging from a mass of thick black swirling grass. The movement of the grass swinging her from one side, then over to the next. Opal flicked her head around, the grass on the walls was scattered sporadically in no real pattern, her arms not long enough to touch the jagged stone walls of the crater. She raced through the centre of the cavity, her feet twitching as if trying to push the breaks on a car. She clenched her teeth and was hanging like a doll in mid-air. There was no doubt that the crater was in charge. A rush of wind slammed into her right-hand side and she veered to the left. Her arms were outstretched and touching the crater wall now. Using lightening quick thinking, she thrust out one arm to grab a clump of animated black grass. She gripped it like a vice and hung on for dear life. She felt herself bounce left to right with the sway of the grass. Swinging into its rhythm. Glancing down, she let go of the big gulp of breath that had filled her now balloon sized lungs.

'Okay, that was crazy, Ruby, we have to start climbing down, are you ready?'

'You cannot be serious' Ruby panted

'Deadly, there is no way we are staying here waiting for death to call. It is too far up. We must go down!'

Ruby wriggled into a different position, the dull ache in her arms getting more pronounced with each moment.

'But it, might, be, bottomless?' she said between breaths.

Opal screwed up her face, the pain in her arms like a thousand needles had been inserted.

'Okay, do you have a better idea?'

Ruby shook her mane of black curls and swallowing hard. She released one foot thrashing it around in the air until it caught the rock beneath. Followed by release of the hand on the same side. She fumbled around trying to find a rock that jutted out just enough that her fingers could hold it. Then she released the other hand and foot, moving at a snail's pace down the wall, but moving all the same. A rush of dust dropped into Opal's eye dislodged by Ruby's white kitten healed slipper. Opal rubbed her eye with one hand *thanks Ruby* she mused. She looked at her dust covered hand, then let out a squeak of panic. Only one hand holding the grass now. She rushed to place the free hand beneath her tummy on the stone wall and dropped her foot to a lower level at the same time. Feeling around with her bare feet to find a sturdy rock to secure herself to. Then she stepped down again and again. Ruby could see the shape of Opal below her, navigating the wall like an experienced climber. Opal had that look that said she had done this a thousand times. Ruby on the other hand had all the confidence and stability of a baby learning to crawl for the first time. She was sure she could see light further down the crevice but wondered if her imagination was playing tricks on her. Opal scanned the wall. It was flatter now and she could not find the next ledge to move to.

'The wall is getting flatter here. I am not sure if I can go any further' she shouted.

Ruby had gained pace and was only a couple of body lengths above. She lunged at the next ledge and was able to shuffle her body a couple of feet but, as she did a large stone dislodged itself from its thousand-year home in the wall and rolled in Opal's direction.

'Look out!' screamed Ruby

Opal spun around, only to see a large boulder rushing towards her. Smash, it struck her cheek bone with a loud crunch. Opal let out an aggrieved groan before floating away from the wall and back into the swirling, space style abyss. The world began spinning at a hundred miles an hour and a wave of nausea rose in her gut. Ruby strained her neck, searching the chasm for a glimpse of Opal who was now a tiny spec in the vastness. Ruby froze at her spot on the wall. A gaggle of thoughts racing through her head, *what should I do, where are the others, I wish I could help*….. And on that thought, her dress started to glow, lighting the dark of the cavity. A warm blush of red, radiating through the thin cotton material of her summer dress. She tentatively released one hand from the wall and reached into her pocket to find her blessed Ruby. She racked her brain trying to recall how to use its magic and what its powers were. This was all very new to her.

'I wish I had some friends to help' she said out loud.

'If you let go of our hair, we will be happy to help?' Said a sweet childlike voice.

Ruby followed the direction of the voice. It was the black grass, it was talking. Then before her very eyes a small grey potato shaped animal popped out of the wall wearing the thick black grass hair she had been so carelessly heaving on her climb down. Its minute suckered illuminous green hands and feet tightly secured to the wall. It had round eyes and a matching shaped mouth, but no visible nose. Quite a peculiar looking creature. Ruby looked across the rock face and could suddenly see thousands of them, half their heads and eyes peeping out and looking in her direction. Their faces were open, almost innocent looking and friendly. Ruby kept very still, like a cat who had been confronted by a ferocious dog. She remembered the Ruby had the ability to turn things into her friend, though she had never tested its powers since first finding it at Braeriach Mountain.

'Thank you and hello, could you please help my friend Opal, she has fallen from the wall and she may be hurt?'

She spat this out all in one hurried breath.

'Of course,' the creature replied. Wrestling the remainder of its body out of the whole in the wall. Its belly getting stuck as it wriggled itself completely free. The others did the same, making a popping sound as they did. A little army of potatoes suckering their way down the wall in front of her very eyes. Until she could not see them anymore.

'Now jump, your friend is safe at the bottom with the others. You must trust us and jump'

Ruby took a deep breath as though she was about to jump into a swimming pool that she could not see, then used her arms to spring her away from the wall. Falling feet first into the darkness. She could not see her own hand in front of her face but felt that the gravity was pulling her further down. Her dress flying high above her waist with the motion. The Ruby still lighting the way like a rose-coloured torch. Just beneath her feet she could make out a kind of landing pad. She was closer still now. It was the potato creatures who were stacked one on top of the other like a giant pile of potato cushions. Opal saw Ruby following and waded through the mass of potato bodies making a clearing for Ruby. Ruby gently fell into the crowd of creatures, cushioned by their light and airy, balloon like figures. On landing safely, she sat upright and saw Opal stepping towards her.

'Thank goodness. You are safe. They say the Sable Witches used magic to create the crater'

Ruby threw her arms around Opal's neck

'I thought I had lost you. How scary was that. Where are we?'

Opal laughed, her familiar deep laugh and slapped Ruby's back.

'Well, when we exited thunder pass, we were definitely in Australia, at the bottom of the world. I recognise the birds and trees anywhere, then we dropped down through the crater, which probably means we are now at the top of the world. I am guessing somewhere in England?'

The potatoes were now back on their tiny sucker feet and crowded around the two girls. Above their heads, they could see a stunning picture postcard scene of craggy mountains, surrounded by a mix of leafless trees and green firs. There was a frosty chill in the air and every breath sent a chain of white air from their lips. Ruby searched her new surroundings. Absorbing its absolute breath-taking beauty.

'It's Scotland'

Ruby and the creatures said in chorus. Followed by a burst of laughter at the uncanny timing of their words.

'How do you know?' Opal asked, hands on hips scouring the landscape.

'I can see Braeriach Mountain. My mother lives here. Let's go'

Opal grabbed her hand and held her in the spot she stood.

'Steady on. Manners please. Thank you for your help kind creatures!' Opal reminded Ruby that they had so much to thank the creatures for.

Ruby looked a little sheepish but was still totally focused on the direction of her mother's house. Opal shrugged in surrender.

'Thank you, guys, come on then Ruby, lead the way!'

The potato creatures waved their suckers in the air, then started to stick their way back up the crater wall.

CHAPTER 7

THE THREE SISTERS

The cool wind negotiated its way inside Rubies dress as she walked. Her body began to tremble as the cold chill reached her skin, but she marched forward, undeterred from her destination. Opal walked quickly tripping and sliding and really struggling to keep up. Her tiny legs occasionally starting to skip a little as she tried to match Ruby's pace. Her bare feet being poked and pricked with every stone and stick she met on the path.

'Stop, this is crazy. Wait a moment!' Opal protested drawing out her Opal from her pocket and holding it to her eye. It didn't need a second prompt. It immediately flashed into action, dressing them both head to toe in floor length white marble faux fur coats, matching hats, gloves, and of course cowboy boots. Opals personal favourite footwear and of course, it must always be white. That is the reason they were named the White Witches after all, so they wore the colour with pride. Opal gave a proud jerk of her head and continued the skippy walk complete with her new trudging cowboy boots! Ruby hardly noticed the change; she was completely focused on her mission until she tripped on a rock. She looked down to see what object dared to get in her path, blocking the route to her beloved mother, only to find a pair of, yes, cowboy boots. She paused for a nano second. Then glanced at Opal with raised eyebrows. Opal gave the famous 'what's the matter' shrug. Ruby responded with a disapproving shake of her head and tramped on. Then, there it was in front of them. That old, tired building she called her home and refuge. She began to perform a clumsy cowboy boot run up the dandelion filled path to the front door. MoCharaid saw her first and rushed towards her rolling across the grass as if someone had kicked the giant stone into life.

'Ruby you are home! We have missed you!' Said her best friend and literal rock. Opal stopped dead in her tracks.

'What is that?' She puzzled pointing in the direction of MoCharaid.

'This is MoCharaid, MoCharaid this is Opal. MoCharaid is a talking magic rock which I found on the mountain when I was a child. You must remember him from my White Witch Sept Ceremony?' MoCharaid gave Opal a hello bump against her ankle. Opal returned the greeting with an even more confused frown, rubbing her forehead. *Definitely had too much sunlight* she thought. It was at that moment that Amber joined the welcome committee. Amber flung open the door and wrapped her arms around Ruby, holding her as though she might never let her go. Ruby felt the warmth of her mother's arms around her and felt the heart ache of her recent ordeals float weightlessly away all at the same time. Charles beamed an affectionate smile at his guests. He was now standing close behind Amber holding two cups of bubbling cream laden hot chocolates.

Opal starred at the chocolate powdered cream floating on top of her hot chocolate. As delicious as it was, it was not a comfort. She was she still chastising herself for listening to Ruby's directions. This is how they had ended up in Scotland when they should have been in Australia by now. She watched the animated conversation between Amber and Ruby. Observing the real expressions of love passing over both of their faces whilst they spoke. Charles (Professor Clapton) perched on a rickety chair in the corner, observing, silent and smiling. They were both passive witnesses of the love so obviously shared between Amber and Ruby. Charles was a little apprehensive to force his way into the conversation. Although he was Ruby's Father, he had to respect that he had not been part of her life until now. This would take a little getting used to for all of them. Opal glanced at the clock on the wall, unsure of the time, or how many days had passed since they had left Validor or how long they had left to save the world. She picked at the polka dot pink pyjamas they had changed into on arriving.

'Would you like me to reheat your chocolate Opal?' Amber asked. She noticed Opal had barely touched it for nearly an hour.

'No thank you Amber. I am not feeling very thirsty. If it is okay with you, I would like to head off to bed?'

She placed the charcoal-coloured cup on the worn oak coffee table. Then stood up, her knees gently knocking the worn oak coffee table as she did. The coffee table suddenly opened its eyes and looked up to the heavens. Somewhat tired of the daily bashing it took from clumsy legs. *As if a coffee table would have eyes* contemplated Opal wearing a half-amused smile. Ruby reached out and touched Opal's thigh.

'Would you like me to show you to your room?' She asked quietly. Opal gave Ruby a cold stare.

'No thank you. If your sense of direction is anything like it was earlier, we might end up in a crater journeying to the centre of the earth' Ruby looked at the floor, her cheeks flushing pink.

'Well, that's harsh. I saved your life by making the potato creatures our friends!' She retorted with a gentle reminder that told Opal she should have a little gratitude.

Opal laughed but was already striding out of the room at full speed.

Amber screwed up her face, a bewildered look creeping across her eye line unsure of what the pair were talking about. She patted the chair next to her on the sofa.

'Potato creatures and craters? Sit down, it sounds like we have so much to talk about!'

Charles hoisted himself up and began collecting the mugs on the coffee table. Then disappeared into the hallway gently closing the door behind him.

Amber could not hide the alarm in her face as she learned of the horror of her daughter's adventures over recent days. She learned Validor her White Witch home and earth was under threat from the Sable Witches, and she felt so powerless to help. She was still very much a victim of her mothers' loss of powers from an exceedingly early age and her magic was the weakest of all the White Witches, but she was still a much-loved family member all the same and had so many lovely memories of meetings at the White Witch coven as she was growing up.

'The only thing I find confusing is where the crater came from and why?' Ruby said her eyes dancing around in a totally bewildered manner as she relived the whole chain of events with her mother.

'Well, that I can answer!' Amber jumped in.

'Sounds like Yowla's magic for sure. She is the master of powerful potions and disease. Quite a formidable set of powers has Sable Witch Yowla. My guess is the Sable Witches knew that Opal was the most likely to know how to find the Jenolan Caves, the Crucible of Doom and Devils Arch. So, they wanted to make sure you didn't get there'.

Once again, she gave Ruby a tender embrace.

'I am only glad that you are here, safe and sound and in one piece'

Ruby placed her arms around her mother's shoulders and gave her a peck on the cheek.

'So am I mother, truly!'

Ruby started to withdraw when she heard a loud whirring sound in her ear. She jumped away from Amber's slender arm and looked around the room. The noise seemed to be coming from the floor beneath her feet. She swept her legs to one side and looked to the dark wood dusty floor. Her mother tried to keep it clean but with each whoosh of the big solid oak front door, a blast of dust would join them in the front room. She was met by two big sapphire blue eyes peering up at her.

'Jasmine!' She shouted.

Jasmine the cat stopped the loud purring and jumped in shock at Ruby's shriek, skidding a little across the highly polished wooden floor as she did. Amber and Ruby laughed whilst Ruby lovingly scooped her up in her arms, pushing her face close to Jasmines and kissing her fluffy white whiskered cheeks. Charles burst in the doorway carrying a tray of tomato plants at a jaunty angle. The soil spilling out onto the floor.

'What happened?' He said wearing a look of genuine concern at all the commotion.

The girls laughed, still stroking Jasmine like they had not seen her for one hundred years. Charles corrected the position of the tray but still looked a little perplexed.

'So, this is what you missed back home Ruby' Giggled Amber.

'Gardening and growing tomatoes plants. Not quite as exciting as your escapades!'

'I like tomatoes' Charles said, as he began carefully straightening one of the stems with his free hand, looking ever so slightly offended.

Amber stroked his cheek affectionately. Ruby and Amber gave each other a knowing glance as if to say, *best he stays in the dark.*

'Me too my love, me too' Amber smiled that soothing smile she always gave that needed no words.

Amber placed her hand around Ruby's shoulder and walked her through the long echoey corridor. Stepping quietly up the stairs towards their bedrooms.

♟♟♟

The sizzling intensity of the Australian sun beat down on the three sisters. Their once quick dance steps slowly grinding to a holt due to their sheer exhaustion. The sisters lived in Ice Valley close to Sable Witch Whitney and were not accustomed to the scalding hot temperatures that Australia is famous for. The Mummy had left hours ago, and Astro and Armando departed shortly after. The three sisters had been completely absorbed in their magic generating dance. They had learned some time ago that the more they moved, the stronger their powers became. It was an important ritual they performed each time they embarked onto any wicked mission. The paradox of this was the sheer elegance and gracefulness of the dance. As evil as the sisters were, they were strikingly exquisite shimmering silver beings and extremely easy on the eye. It was not difficult to deduce how things became seduced by them before becoming the victim of their evil deeds. They instinctively knew when it was time to stop prancing, and that they had a literal belly full of wicked magic. This time, still holding hands, they raised them to the sky, tilting their slender necks so their faces face the sun in all its glory. They started to take steps forward, making the circle they had formed much, much smaller, until they were brushing against one another's celestial type bodies and as their bodies finally met, they merged into a silver bullet like shape which launched high into the vast sky like a rocket, disappearing higher and higher, as they flew the first few miles towards their next evil mission.

♟♟♟

Amber stroked Rubies hair maternally at the bedroom door and gave her a light peck on the cheek.

'It is lovely to have you here again' She said softly.

'It is lovely to be here mother' She smiled, opening the bedroom door gently so as not to wake Opal and as she did, there was a spectacular crack of thunder and the light in the bedroom began to flash. Ruby began to shake uncontrollably with the shock of moving from such a peaceful night, to this. Amber heaved her away from the doorway and stepped inside. A rush of wind tried to fight her back out of the room. Amber used all the strength she could find to fight her way back in. The room was brightly lit by something, but what was it? The room seemed to be empty. She pushed against the wind, another three steps forward, then another until she could see the window was wide open and slamming open, then shut repeatedly. She dragged herself through the pressure of the

S.E.Aitken

wind to reach it and leaning out through the window she gave a pained scream. A bedraggled Charles appeared at the doorway.

'My goodness, what on earth is going on?' He panicked

Amber spun around and began shouting as loud as she could through the howl of the wind and slamming windows. Her face as white as paper.

'It's Opal, the three sisters have her in the garden!'

Charles blinked and gulped in fear. He had no real power, but he could not let his family come to any harm, he saw this as his new role in life. He threw his shabby green dressing gown to the floor like a mild-mannered man on a mission.

'Stay here, I will deal with this!' He said authoritatively, wagging a crooked shaky finger at Amber and Ruby.

He bounded down the stairs, through the messy kitchen complete with used hot chocolate mugs and pans. He battered them around trying to find the back door key. It was hanging on the wall he forgot. Wrestling it into the lock, he released the door and tip toed into the garden.

'No Charles!' Wailed Amber from the top of the stairs.

'Ruby stay here' she said gripping Ruby's shoulders in a motherly way. Ruby was not of a mind to do much more. She was still stood trembling in the bedroom doorway, frozen to the spot. Amber took the same path as Charles except stopping quickly to grab her magic cloak from the broom cupboard. The scene Amber met in the garden was horrifying, the three sisters were circling Opal, using their strange voices to echo a thousand times around her ears. Opal was gripping them, as if shielding them from harm. The light they had seen in the bedroom was the shine of the three sisters translucent power filled figures filtering through the bedroom window from the garden. The dance of the sisters was much more sinister than that they had performed in the forest earlier that day. It was much more aggressive and angular. The faces of the sisters moved from that of an angelic child to the face of a demon with black eyes and a blood red tongue interchangeably. Charles stood motionless, looking around him for something to cause a distraction or perhaps a weapon to scare these things away. He scratched his head, anxiously, running his fingers through his unkempt wild flash of grey hair as if doing this might bring him the answer. Before it came to him, Amber's face was in front of him. She quickly raised the cloak throwing it over his head. He was gone. Completely invisible. She breathed out a sigh of release. *Okay, next Opal* she thought rotating around to face the direction of Opal and the three crazy sisters. The strange and eerie sound of the sister's words sending shocks into her ears. It was like they were saying something, then a thousand echoing voices repeated that same something. The words were not in a language she was familiar with. They were at least fifty paces away. She needed to find a way to drag Opal out of the circle. She cast her white fluffy slippers to one side and began to sprint towards her. In less than ten seconds she was close. A stark lightning bolt light flashed again, and she was immediately thrown to the floor clutching her eyes the bright light had distorted her sight. She could not see. It was like all the cameras in the world had flashed together in unison right into her eyes. She felt sharp needle like pains as her eyes tried to adjust. She could just make out the sisters still flapping their arms and pirouetting around Opal in a crazed manic dance frenzy. The slender nymph like heavenly creatures they once were, had now turned into silver haired hag like beings. It seemed the more power they used, the older they grew. Amber squinted holding one hand like a salute above her eyebrow searching for Opal. It was then she saw her, and so did Ruby who had made her way to the window and was leaning out. Opal was a cold, solid, motionless figurine in the garden. Her angry fearless expression perfectly preserved in ice on her face. Amber touched her feet managing to duck the fireworks of light still being thrown around the garden by the sisters. She looked up to see the sisters were now turning into the direction of Ruby in the window. Amber managed to scramble across the floor towards them. She reached into her pocket and pulled out her Amber. Gave it a gentle kiss. Then with the next lightening flash threw her Amber into the shock of light. Then there was a last thunderous crack followed by, nothing. There was silence. The sisters suddenly stopped their manic dance, then they all raised one arm, then the other, like totally disorientated ragdolls. They looked at their hands as if they did not recognise themselves. Then began to walk calmly away into the darkness of the forest.

'Mother, are you and Dad okay?' Ruby hollered.

'I am okay, Dad will be too, once I remove my cloak' She muttered furiously rummaging through the grass to retrieve her Amber. She found it embedded in a lump of grass. She cradled it affectionately and began to polish it on her pyjama pants all the time thinking how nice it was to hear Ruby call Charles's dad.

'I didn't know you could still use magic mother?' she panted.

'I have a little, gets me out of a few fixes, sadly it will not get Opal back. That will take powers we do not have I am afraid. Don't worry, she is safe here until the others can help'

Ruby did not like the thought of a frozen Opal in her mother's garden, but at least they could see she would come to no further harm if she were here. Amber stumbled across to Charles and lifted off the cloak. Charles sat mesmerized for a moment, then began to scratch his head again.

'What happened?' He said still a little dazed.

'Nothing for you to worry about dear. Come along, let us get you into the house' Amber gently lifted his elbow to help him onto his feet. Charles was too disorientated to ask any more questions. He dotingly linked his arm through hers and walked back into the house.

Hours passed before Ruby felt her eyes begin to surrender to the day's events. She had been trying to keep them open just in case there were any more uninvited guests joining them this evening. Her fatigue finally beat her, and she started to drift away, but not for long.

'Ruby, Ruby' repeated a familiar deep male voice. Ruby opened one eye to see Emperor Zilante, floating weightlessly in her room. His green cloak sweeping the floor as he hoovered gently above her. His long stripy beard trailing at the end of her bed covers. For a moment she thought she was dreaming, but the cold of the night air creeping through the gaps in the window frame were a chilly reminder that she was not.

'Your Majesty, I mean, Emperor Zilante. Is that you?'

'Yes, Ruby, it is. I have something important to say. I need you to be strong now and continue your journey without Opal. You must get to the Crucible of Doom in Devils Arch before the Sable Witches do and rescue the Diamond. Do you think you can you do this?' He raised an eyebrow, arms firmly crossed high across his regal chest. It did not feel like a question to Ruby. It was more like a command.

'I, I think so. I mean, I still do not truly know how to use my Ruby, or how to get there but, I know I must try'

She answered as honestly as she could.

'Good, okay then. You must now find your way back to the Crater and climb back through it. It is the only way' He insisted. Then continued.

'One more thing. Daylin, and Daylin only, must take the Diamond to Lucas Cave and place it between the gap between the magic stalagmite and stalactite into the Precipice of Peace. This will cleanse the Diamond of evil powers it may have absorbed whist in the Sable Witches custody and restore peace in Validor and on earth' Ruby could not comprehend why it should be Daylin but was too afraid to ask.

'But how do I find Daylin and how do I find any of those places you speak of?'

There was no reply. As quickly as Zilante ghost like figure had appeared before her, it vanished into nothingness.

'Emperor, please, HOW DO I EVEN FIND THE CRATER!' She bellowed. On hearing Ruby's shouts, Amber came crashing through the door in a frenzy with a broom in her hand, ready to attack the next intruder.

'What, what crater, are you okay?' She said all a fluster.

'It was Emperor Zilante, he visited me. Said something about finding the crater' she slurred in a half a sleep voice.

'Ruby, you must get some sleep. You are hallucinating. Your lack of sleep is giving you vivid dreams my love' Amber reassured her trying to encourage her to get some more rest.

Ruby yawned and nodded, lay her head back down on the starch white pillow and as her dark curls dropped beside her face. She then fell into a deep slumber.

The next morning, Ruby ate her marmalade coated toast sitting close to the ice statute that was once Opal in the garden. Although the cold from the concrete step had begun to seep through her white trousers, she was reluctant to move away from Opal. She wondered if Opal could hear or see them. MoCharaid sat dutifully beside her on the step.

'Mo, I know mother thinks I was dreaming, but I really did see Emperor Zilante' she implored.

'I believe you Ruby, but what would he want with you?'

'He said I must find the crater. The crater Opal and I travelled through to get here. It is the only way back to Australia and to the Crucible of Doom in Devils Arch'

MoCharaid dropped off the step and rolled around her feet, as if pacing.

'I see, but why on earth would you want to go there?'

'I must find the Diamond before the Sable Witches have the chance to place it on the Crucible of Doom in Devils Arch, and if I don't, well if I don't' she paused to catch her breath, fighting back the tears. She dropped her plate of toast to the side of her and began to sob uncontrollably into her dainty hands. The tears flowing between her fingers and showering MoCharaid as he had bumped onto her lap.

'Earth or Validor will be destroyed' she said, in a quivering whisper of a voice.

'Please do not cry Ruby. I know I am not much help, but if there is one thing I do know about it is rocks, craters, and mountains. I can help?'

Ruby lifted her head and stopped crying. Her face slowly breaking into a sad smile.

'Would you Mo. Thank you. You are my hero!' She stroked his rock like head adoringly. *What would she do without him?* She thought thankfully.

She stood up and collecting her empty plate, sauntered into the kitchen. The back door had been ajar, and Charles had heard the conversation. He busily rinsed dishes in the sink with his back to Ruby. Placing a clean dripping plate on the rack he said.

'You could always get the plane?'

Ruby gave a polite smile. Charles was so new to the ways of the Witches. She placed a hand on his shoulder and leaned forward, giving him a gentle kiss on his weather worn skin.

'Thank you, Father. Although I think that might take far too long. I am afraid by the time I arrive. It would be too late'

Charles nodded a little sad that he could not help but secretly still glad she had called him father.

CHAPTER 8

THE WEREWOLFS DINNER

Armando the Werewolf crunched through the forest in his hap hazard carefree way. Sniffing at tree trunks and grabbing at the odd white parquets as they passed over his head. Boredom was beginning to set in. His thick fur clad paws caked in the mud they had collected from the forest floor. He stopped and sniffed the air. He sniffed again. There was a feint smell of flowers floating on the breeze, but not the usual smell of Australian forest natives. No this was something, far stronger, less familiar. Less earthly. He drew in another draft of the scent into his highly tuned nostrils until his mind accurately identified the scent. It was the smell of Validor Lotus. Morganite's favourite flower for making healing potions.

Morganite dabbed the ointment on Moonstone's ankle which had now roasted to a crisp in the heat of the sun.

Moonstone moaned as it made contact with her tight red skin. Then sighed as the white milky liquid found its way through it and cooled it down. The heat in her skin slowly reducing with each second that passed. Even the redness had disappeared. Morganite replaced the lid and placed it back inside one of the leather pouches in his armour. Moonstone stood upright, swaying a little as she did. The sun had totally drained her of energy, and they had walked for what seemed like miles. They both gave each other a look and a nod. Too exhausted for words but knowing they must push on if they were going to reach Devils Arch before the Sable Witches. They shuffled forward, hardly able to lift one foot in front of the other. Taking comfort from the fact that the sun had dropped behind the trees now and darkness was upon them.

Armando could hear the crunch of grass in front of him, he knew he must be close to Morganite. The distinctive smell of Validor Lotus, the unmistakable sound of White Witch feet meeting the crispy grass. The light of day had slowly diminished and only a balmy breeze remained. Night-time crept in and the sound of a choir of a million crickets filled the air. Armando lifted his head to face the full moon illuminating the sky. It was like a giant pepper mint coloured glass globe, filled with the light of a zillion fireflies. He opened his jaws and took a deep breath. He released a breath at the same time as making the loudest most haunting, wolf like howl.

'OOOOOOOwwwwwwww, OOOOOOwwwwww!'

He stretched his legs, pushing his bottom upwards like a dog would, his wolf like body stiff from the walk. All four feet burned from the baking soil they had traipsed across. He lay down on the floor under the canopy of an apparently incredibly old tree. It stood strong and proud, almost boosting that it had managed to stand up to all the Australian elements for hundreds of years, yet he struggled to survive the day. He rested his long limp legs on the ground.

'Did you hear that?' Morganite sat erect on the floor where they had stopped. His head tilted to one side, eyes searching the dark sky.

Moonstone nodded and gulped, too afraid to speak. She linked her arm through Morganite's for comfort.

'That was the howl of Armando the werewolf. I would know that sound anywhere' Morganite was now on his feet turning and leaning from side to side, peering through the trees. Except he could see nothing in the darkness. He turned to face Moonstone, shrugging his shoulders and waving his hands.

'Cannot see anything, no need to...' But before he could finish, he was splayed on the floor face down. He felt the weight of a barrel of bricks on top of him and was fighting for every breath.

'Worry' he finished his sentence with a groan.

Moonstone scuffled to her feet, walking backwards on her hands like a crab. Her feet could not move quickly enough for her. She was desperate to create a distance between herself and the brawl that was happening right in front of her very eyes. A wolf greater in height than Morganite and herself combined, had launched itself from the shadows and onto Morganites back. It was clad with shaggy dirty brown fur, its tongue hung from the side of its mouth, dripping with drool onto the floor.

'Oh no, oh no, I don't know how to tell you this but, there is a, well, a massive wolf on your BACK!'

Armando dug his claws deeper into Morganite's shoulders, pinning him flatly to the floor.

'You don't say' Morganite pushed out the words as best as he could, the weight of Armando had shrunk his lung capacity to zero. He eventually wrestled his arms free and began to roll the two of them like a couple of quarrelling crocodiles and each time they rolled, Morganite gripped Armando's head and tried to slam it to the floor, but Armando resisted it with his strong athletic neck keeping his head just enough distance from the ground to stay out of trouble. Then Armando was on top again, grinning menacingly.

'You don't say' imitated Armando, smiling that, *I am pleased with myself* grin.

'Oy, get off my friend, you, you ugly beast!' Moonstone protested.

'Oy, get off my friend, you, you ugly beast!' Armando mirrored with the best girly expression he could muster. Showing how he had clearly mastered the art of White Witch impressions amongst others.

Morganite writhed his heavy-set body desperately trying to escape. Moonstone tried to help and grabbed the fur on Armando's neck, yanking it with every ounce of strength she could recover.

'Stand back! Stand back or!' Morganite said with a muffled tense voice. Armando's jaws were now wide open, almost unhinged, like a snake trying to swallow something far greater than itself. Morganite's face was sideways on, with only one seeing eye and that eye that was watching his dear friend Moonstone sliding down Armando's throat headfirst. He was swallowing her whole. Morganite could see her pass into his torso, still in the same form. Her shape the same as it was when she stood close by, only moments ago.

Moonstone slid down the blood vessel passageway that was Armando's stomach. It looked like a roadmap of hell. Her body and arms tightly compressed together. It was a glossy, slimy, skiddy pathway. She was shooting through a mass of spaghetti long Pink tubes until abruptly coming to a halt. Then she was catapulted into a great red cavity, making the sound of a cork popping from a bottle of Champagne. She shook her head, *where am I?* She was rising and falling as though seated on a bouncy castle full of heavy weight boxers. There was a sudden Whoosh coming from the direction of the spaghetti tubes and POP, out dropped a slime covered Morganite. He had also joined the water slide from hell. It was then a dose of reality set in for both of them. Armando had devoured both of them, whole.

'As I was saying before, stand back or…. he will eat you' Morganite said sarcastically, but calmly. He tried to shake off the dripping saliva goo from his hands. They were both moving with the rise and falling motion of Armando's stomach walls. It felt like being on the very top of a mound of jelly.

'Sorry?' Moonstone smiled sweetly, her eyelashes batting in an endearing way.

'Now what do we do?' She asked.

'Nothing we can do I am afraid. My magic does not work in here. I could have escaped but did not want to leave you there on your own, so I got close to him so he would see me and eat me too'

Moonstone looked ashamedly down. She leant forward contemplating a thank you kiss, but then changed her mind. Not wanting to be tangled up in the green gloop dripping down Morganite's cheek. Then Moonstone's jaw set indignantly. She was not going to take this lying down and she could not believe that Morganite would quit so easily. Whispering into her hands she repeated the magic spell she heard Pearl used so many times before. 'Lightania Menanca Portaya' Out jumped the familiar magic bright light. The bauble of light the White Witches would usually use to travel to and from the White Witch Coven. It would transfer them into a tiny spec of light which meant they could travel unnoticed by the Sable Witches. Instinctively the light consumed her, reducing her to a tiny dot like flicker. Morganite yawned and shook his head as she started to float upwards from the pink sticky stomach lining back through the opening she popped from. She began to fly up the tangled knot of intestines in exactly the opposite direction to the way she had travelled. She was so light; she was sure Armando would not know she was on her way out. She reached the top of his throat and could see the back of his mouth. His sharp jagged teeth perched at each side like lethal weapons. His enormous ruddy tongue flapping up and down. Moonstone dived around it, as it was becoming a little unpredictable. Its wave like motion almost caught her twice. She waited until she could see a dot of light. This was the signal she needed to show his mouth may be open, just enough for her to fly through. Then there it was, the moment she had been waiting for. A tiny speck of light visible through a gap in his yellow stained rotten teeth. Her heart pounded in her chest like a herd of wild elephants, she decided, now was the time to make a break for it, elephants, and all. Except moments later she found herself spiralling down uncontrollably, back into the depths of the pit like stomach of this evil beast. Her head in a dizzy spin, and her own stomach somersaulting up and down. It was quite nauseating. She desperately tried to make sense of what had happened. She had made it to the opening, only to be met by two sharp claws that teasingly flicked her backwards into this black hole abyss. Armando knew she was there and had thwarted her seemingly amateur magic attempts to flee. Flicking her back into his being like an annoying fly. She bounced back down at Morganite's side. He was in the same position as when she had left. He opened one eye.

'Like I said. Nothing we can do' He said in a smug manner.

'Like I said. Nothing we can do' she imitated sticking her tongue out like a scolded child and waggling her head at the same time.

'Anyway, what is this thing we are inside? Who is he? What is he?'

He lay back, propping his hands behind his head.

'Moonstone may I introduce Armando. Armando this is Moonstone' He joked.

'He is Armando the Werewolf. A Sable Witch creation. Now, get some sleep, it is going to be a long wait before we are found' With that, he flipped onto his side not wanting to waste any more energy talking.

CHAPTER 9

JOURNEY TO THE CENTRE
OF THE EARTH

Ruby held her mother like her life depended on it. The thought of never returning was fuelling the clinging bear hug she was inflicting on her. If Opal had been with her, she was sure she would get there safely. Now her confidence was significantly less. She slowly and reluctantly began to release her grip and placed both hands on each of her mother's pale cheeks. Looking into her eyes to reach her heart. There were no words.

Amber tried to comfort her, noticing the fear in her daughter's eyes.

'Hey, hey, hey, it is going to be okay Ruby. We White Witches are well protected. Do not lose faith. Please?' Amber smiled warmly.

Ruby nodded, afraid that any attempt to speak would result in a waterfall of tears. Shuffling between her mother and Charles, she planted a light kiss on Charles cheek, then reached down to stroke Jasmine who was rotating around their feet in her usual morning ritual, oblivious to the sadness around her. Ruby gently picked up Mo and placed him in her old battered, leather school satchel, she had been repairing it through the night especially for this purpose. Mo looked up, smiling reassuringly, and Ruby returned a thankful smile. They reached the gate of the house, closing it carefully behind them. It had seen better years and recently, every slam threatened its very existence. Mo started to rattle around in the bag and Ruby could feel the vibrations on her hip. She lifted the flap and glanced inside to check Mo was alright.

'If you let me out, I can speed things up a little for us?' Mo said eagerly.

Ruby cradled him in her hands and raised him from the satchel. Dropping him lightly to the ground next to her feet. He rolled over towards the tip of her toes.

'Stand on me' he asked.

Ruby did not like the sound of standing on her dear friend, but his big eyes looked to be pleading with her and she did not want to offend. She placed both feet on his body, like she was treading on an eggshell.

'Hold on tight' he winked. Then he began to roll at a phenomenal pace, taking Ruby completely by surprise. She desperately struggled to keep her feet on top of him. This took quite some technique; it was like balancing both feet on a super powered football. The ground moved beneath them so quickly, she began to feel a little dizzy. They were travelling at around one hundred miles per hour now. Then two hundred. They gained ground very quickly, hurtling over fields and dirt tracks, dodging rocks, branches and sticks with effortless precision.

Ruby lifted her arms out, feeling the rush of the wind through her fingers and hair. She had never felt so free.

'This is amazing!' She laughed.

Mo responded with another friendly wink and ploughed on, zooming and zipping through obstacles, and hurdles like a teenager on a computer game. This went on for hours. Ruby's legs began to ache from trying to stay balanced on top of Mo. Her feet were a little sore from gripping him with her toes through her white ballet slippers. She tentatively lifted one foot, then placed it back down, then lifted the other, trying to provide them a little relief from the abrasive surface of Mos body. She wobbled a little as she tried to regain balance. As she did, Mo came to an unexpected stand still, throwing Ruby to the ground in front of him. Ruby dusted her white jeans down.

'Sorry you had to stop Mo; I was struggling to stay on. My legs grew weary'

'Oh, no Ruby, I stopped because we are in the right place. We have found the crater!'

Ruby pushed her mouth to one side of her bewildered face.

'But wait, how do you know?

'Watch, I will roll across the crack so you can trace it better' Mo began to role at a snail's pace this time across the ground. Ruby could see a very feint crack across the soil, and the more she inspected it, the further it seemed to go.

'How did you know it was here?' she asked.

'I have been roaming this land for many years. I know a new crack when I see one. Now, we just need to get it to re-open' No sooner had the words left him, had he started to bounce up and down on the floor. Banging and thudding with the force of a herd of rhinoceroses. He relentlessly pounded the floor. Ruby twisted her face in objection. Not accustomed to displays of violence from her dear friend, but she knew it to be necessary. Then, without warning there was an ear-splitting recognisable sound. They felt the tremor of the earth shaking below them. Ruby remembered the very same feeling before falling into the colossus crevice with Opal only a day earlier and sure enough, moments later, the crack in the floor had resurfaced. Ruby concentrated hard on the direction the crack was travelling in, determined not to end up falling in unexpectedly. Mo did the same, he was on super power, successfully weaving and dodging the line of the crack. Eventually, the booming noise came to an end. Ruby slumped to the ground next to a dizzy Mo. Mo's eyes were rolling a little as though he was still reeling from the somewhat paranoid dance he just enacted. Ruby wheezed in and out, quite lost for breath after her exhilarating game of dodge the crack. She closed her eyes enjoying the momentary peace.

'Mo, Mo… is that you?' An elderly male voice said. Mo, also with eyes closed, opened one of them cautiously. He stared in total disbelief at who was standing in front of him.

'Dad?'

'Is that you?' Mo stammered.

Mo's mind was in total turmoil. He cascaded it back to the bedtime story his grandmother would often tell him. For a child rock, it was such a heart wrenching story. Mainly because it was true, and it involved his Mother and Father, and although he felt sad when he heard it, It was also the only time he felt truly close to them. He began to tell Ruby the story. Many years ago, minutes after he was born, the Sable Witches had burst into their loving family home and kidnapped his Mother and Father. A bloody battle ensued. They bounced their rock like bodies off the walls in the cavern. Bounding from one to the next, then the floor, frantically trying to avoid the evil, mouldy nailed grip of the Sable Witches. Sadly, they failed. The Sable Witches used their power to create a magic vacuum which sucked them into a crate. They then bolted it with a lock and key. His Mother and Father were never to be seen again. It seemed, the Sable Witches had learned that Mo's family held the Ruby, and that they intended to return it to the White Witches. They thought by kidnapping Mo's Mother and Father, this would mean the Ruby could never be returned. Ambers family would never have their White Witch powers reinstated to their former strength prior to Ambers Mother Sylvia (Ruby's grandmother) losing her magic silver locket to the Pixies. She had been punished by the White Witch coven and her powers reduced. However, what the Sable Witches did not know is, that his Mother and Father now had a child. Amid all the commotion. His Grandmother, who lived with his parents, had been wise enough to hide Mo in a blanket under her rock bed until the Sable Witches had returned to Validor. Mo was lovingly raised and cherished by his Grandmother and when Mo was a young adult, she passed the Ruby to him. His grandmother asked Mo to fulfil the wishes of his mother and Father and send it back to its rightful owner, Ruby. So there Mo patiently sat on that bleak Braeriach mountain side, until Ruby came, and the rest, as they say, is history. Mo had no real memories of his Mother and Father, but his home had been filled with their pictures etched on the cavern walls, and there was no mistaking his Father's trademark, bushy, handlebar moustache. Mo finished his story and Ruby gave a sad sigh. She had never really known how Mo and his family had sacrificed their own family, to keep Ruby and the rest of Validor safe. She looked at the floor, both appreciative and ashamed. *Nobody should ever have to sacrifice their family*, she thought.

Mo's dad was standing in front of them now.

'Yes Mo, yes, it is. As soon as I saw those eyes, I knew it was you. You have your Mothers eyes!'

Mo and his Dad rolled over to one another and started to knock against each other affectionately, rock to rock. Ruby looked on. She placed her hand under her chin, it was a remarkably touching reunion.

'Dad, I thought you were dead?'

'So did we, the Sable Witches took us and launched us into the centre of the earth's core hoping that we would never return, but we met a whole new community, who took us in and made us part of it. We dared not try to find our way back because we did not want to put you or Grandma at risk' they continued to knock together in an excited manner. Ruby coughed, trying to get their attention.

'You mean the Potato creatures with black hair. I met them when I last passaged through?'

Mo's Father chortled.

'I can see why you might call them that. They do look a little like potatoes. They are called Nickelnuggles because they live in the earth's core, but yes.'

They all laughed together.

'Come Mo, your mother will be so pleased to see you!'

Mo took a roll back and suddenly became very sombre and subdued. He looked at Ruby, then at his Father as if choosing between them. A look of apprehension crossing his grey rock face.

'Father I would so love to spend some time with you, but I must travel with Ruby to Australia through the earth core. That is how I came to be here and…'

Ruby lightly placed her hand over his tiny mouth to quickly quieten him.

'It's okay Mo, you have done enough. You must stay here with your family. I would not have it any other way. If the Nickelnuggles can help me up the core, the same way as they helped me down, that would be all I need!'

Ruby saw her opportunity to repay her families debt to Mo's family and she was not going to miss it. Mo did not change expression. He saw himself as Ruby's guardian angel in some way, so leaving her was not sitting comfortably with him. He went to speak again, and Ruby placed both hands across his little mouth for the second time.

'Please Mo, let me do this one thing for you this time?'

Mo rubbed against her leg in a sign of appreciation. Then rolled back to his Father's side.

'Dad, is that okay, can I stay here with you?'

Mo's

Dad give him a playful bump.

'Mo, I would not have it any other way, and Ruby, of course, my friends and I will help you back to the top of the core. That would be our pleasure?'

Ruby was a tad afraid of taking the long hike, especially without Mo, but she knew it was the right thing to do. Just watching the two of them together brought a lump to her throat. She could not imagine a life without her own parents and wanted Mo to know what having a family felt like. She smiled a cheerful smile to hide the wave of fear growing in her tummy. Mo rolled back to her feet.

'Goodbye Ruby, I will never forget you. I hope to see you again one day?'

Ruby gulped, stifling back the increasing urge to burst into a river of tears. She never thought she would be saying goodbye to her dear friend.

'Promise you will visit sometimes. Bring your family to mothers for a holiday?'

Mo blinked yes, tears brimming in the well of his eyes, unable to speak himself. Ruby gave a quick unemotional nod before turning her back to hide her sadness. This is something she must do for Mo, after all, he had looked after her family all his life.

'Lead the way!' She said wearing the biggest fake smile she could manage.

CHAPTER 10

TROLL MAGIC

Alex and Pearl sat in the very same place Opal and Ruby had sat some time earlier, although they did not know this at the time. Their skin starting to glow crimson in the relentless Australian sun. They were both sticky with sweat because of their own adventure, dodging the Dark Shadows in Thunder Pass. Alex beamed at Pearl in total elation that they had both lived to tell the tale. Pearl plucked a pink flower which was bravely sticking its head out from amongst the grass. Something she would not usually be appreciative of, but, like Alex, the sense of relief she felt made her grateful for everything. Well almost everything. Everything, except Alex himself.

'I thought we might never make it!' Alex said, grinning from ear to ear.

S.E.Aitken

Pearl gave him a stony stare

'Well, we nearly didn't, thanks to you' she spat. Alex frowned.

'Really, the way I saw things, I saved you. You should be grateful. If it were not for me dragging you through, you would still be in there!'

Pearl raised her eyebrows in a matter-of-fact way.

'You keep telling yourself that. I remember you getting tangled up with one and me pulling you away, right at the very end?'

'Maybe, but we would not have got to the end had it not been for me?'

Alex looked at her in disbelief. He had a totally different recollection of events and was offended that Pearl refused to acknowledge that she had been rescued. He knew there it was a waste of effort to fight with her. There was nothing that would change her mind. Pearl could be a stubborn single-minded individual at the best of times, but it didn't stop him relieving his version of their adventure in his own mind, not quite believing what had happened to them. Especially the point when Pearl was trapped by a crowd of shadow's arms and he had to use his small magic dagger, tucked in his armour, to slash them away. It was an incredibly special dagger. No other dagger could literally cut through shadows and ghosts. These usually transparent beings were typically resistant to any human or White Witch weapons, but not his dagger. He reached into his pocket and retrieved his dagger, stroking it lightly, as if he were thanking it.

'Sometimes, I think you need to use your Pearl of truth to make you tell the truth' He mumbled. He then reached over as though he was trying to grab it from the pouch where she held it in her armour. She retaliated with a swift knock of his

140

hand away from her. She didn't want to give him another opportunity to do it again, so she hastily stood up. Her legs still a little unsteady from the Lightening Pass ride. Straightening her helmet, she slowly stepped away from him.

'Oh Pearl, don't be silly. You need to stay close so we can look after each other' he begged. She waved her hand in the air dismissively, and continued to stamp forward, flicking her glossy long black locks of hair in an act of defiance. She began to walk towards the trees close by and, as she did, she noticed a sign 'Frenchs Forest'. She lifted her head in the air, feeling more confident by the minute. *This should be easy, everywhere is sign posted, who needs Alex* she supposed. A small part of her wrestled with the idea of summonsing a magic super car, but she eventually cancelled that notion out of her mind. She did not want to bring too much attention to herself on earth. It would be akin to dropping tiny White Witch breadcrumbs which would lead the Sable Witches directly to her.

Eighteen kilometres' later, a bedraggled Pearl flopped down into the soft welcoming sand of Freshwater Beach. She pushed her hands deep into the sand, its warm inviting texture as if sheltering them from the scorching heat. If she had not sat, she was sure she would have collapsed. The sea was gently lapping her bare toes. Her boots lined up next to her. She removed them as soon as she reached the beach. She had feet full of blisters and aching calves. She could go no further. Her stomach had started to complain of hunger, and she was unsure of how to find food. For a brief second, she wondered if she had been right to leave Alex, he may be waiting for her. How long would he wait, she contemplated, now starting to worry a little about his safety. The beach had some small coves that looked like a place she could perhaps shelter and sleep later. She placed her hands into the sea to wash of the debris of sand that refused to leave her hand. She glanced over at the beautiful cove and wondered if she could cultivate the last ounce of energy from her over worked muscles to reach it and as she began to move, she heard a voice.

'I find if you meditate it takes away the burn of the sun, at least momentarily' It said in a caring and compassionate manner.

She traced the direction of the voice to a strange small man with a pot belly, standing close by, it was Astro the troll, servant to the Sable Witches. Of course, Pearl had no idea who he was, so she innocently engaged him in conversation. It had been hours since she had anyone to talk to.

'Yes, meditation is also my favourite thing to do, I am afraid it probably would not help. I have been wearing this heavy armour for days. It is starting to chaff and is so uncomfortable, I think any mediation now would not provide much relief'

Astro nodded sympathetically.

'I see, that sucks. Well, my sister is not too far up the beach and has a spare beach rap if you would like to loan it?' He said generously. Pearl was so desperate to get out of the heavy armour, she lost all regard for her own personal safety.

'That would be lovely, thank you for your kindness, but I cannot walk any further'

'That is okay, I can carry you on my back. Let's get you sorted. What do you say?' He held out his hand as though she was the oldest and dearest friend he had ever had. Then guided her up from the sandy shore. She limply passed her arms around Astro's neck, wrapped her lithe legs around his waist, and they began to walk a comedic hobble along the sand. Pearl's legs dangled close to his ankles. She was far too big to be on Astro's back but, right now, as exhausted as she was, this felt like travelling first class. Astro had been truthful when he said it was not too far. It was only a matter of minutes before he was dropping her feet back onto solid ground.

'We are here!' He announced.

They were at the opening to a small grey rock cave, tucked away amongst the dunes. He stepped inside the entrance, excitedly beckoning to Pearl to join him. A little voice in her head was telling her she should not go into a cave with a stranger, but once again, she disregarded everything she knew just to be able to take off the dead weight body armour she had been humping around for, what felt like an eternity.

'Thank you... I did not get your name?' she murmured as she began to wrestle the helmet from her head. He turned to face her after removing his own shoes. Then gave a mean smirk.

'My name is Astro the troll and you are Pearl, The White Witch'

Pearl froze for a second with her helmet still in mid-air. She knew the name, often travellers to Compassion Crystal Mountain would tell her horrific tales of the beastly things this troll had done to them. She tried to stay very still, and perfectly calm.

'Well, thank you Astro for all your trouble. If you could bring me your sisters wrap, I will be on my way' She said, pretending she had no knowledge of who he was and what he is capable of. Astro looked a little confused.

'Oh, yes of course, just a second' he faltered on his words and began to walk to the door. Pearl followed him with her eyes, adrenaline began to pump through her veins giving her that extra boost of energy she needed to escape. As soon as he was no longer in sight, she pulled on her boots, fastened on her helmet, and began to creep back towards the entrance. She was only two footsteps away and could almost see the shore when Astro boomed in a menacing voice.

'Going somewhere?'

Pearl did not waste time trying to reply, she tried to walk faster, but her heavy boots cut into her feet, and it hurt so much when she tried to increase the pace. Suddenly, he was gripping her neck and trying to drag her to the floor. Pearls neck diameter seemed to be shrinking to the size of a girl's bangle in his hands. The air passage in her throat beginning to close, she fought for every breath. Her back thrust sharply backwards with the weight of Astro swinging on her neck. She knew she must escape his grip somehow before it was too late. She pushed her hands under his arms and with a swift crack karate type move, she had released his vice like grip. Her neck throbbed and pulsed. He had certainly left his mark. Deep trails of troll fingerprints, glowing purple on her neck. She took off before he could think, almost losing her footing in the momentary panic, in a scuttling frenzy towards the cave entrance. She was seconds away, when there was a loud twanging type sound and she could just make out a golden pitchfork, passing her head, only millimetres away. She felt the breeze as it brushed past her cheek. It gave her just enough warning and time to make a quick swerve to the left to avoid it. The fork came to a crash landing directly in front of her, reverberating as it struck deep into the ground. Astro flashed past her gurgling and chanting in a strange, unrecognisable language. He seized the fork and yanked it from the floor with both hands. His first attempt to retrieve it failed. Pearl squinted past him, wondering if she could get past whilst he was distracted. He tried again, this time wrenching on the fork with such gusto and brute force, it had no choice but to release. He gave out a groan as he fell backwards onto the floor, fork in hand. As he did, fountains of water emerged through the piercings on the floor, gallons and gallons of sea water started to pump into the floor of the cave. Pearl decided it was now or never. She made a final run for the cave exit. Astro was still chanting, eyes rolled back into his head, the complete whites of his eyes now on display. His pupils no longer visible, just white egg like cold eyes. Pearl took the final step to the cave exit, then Astro appeared in front of her. It made no sense; her mind could not comprehend how he arrived there so sharply. As quickly as she thought this, he was gone. There was a tap on her shoulder. She flicked her black hair around, turning to face the direction of the tap.

'Boo!' Astro laughed hysterically who had suddenly reappeared behind her. Then disappeared in front of her very eyes. Once more, she felt a thud on the back of her head from a rock that had smashed her from behind. It dropped to the floor and rolled away. She twisted around to see where the rock came from. An arrogant faced Astro leaned on the cave wall behind her. He shrugged, widening his eyes in an innocent, *it was not me expression*. Pearl's head was baffled, what was this strange magic that seemed to be transporting him from one part of the room to the next, in the blink of an eye. Whatever it was, Astro was enjoying it, and he especially liked the constant look of terror on Pearl's face. He raised his hands in the air and clapped his hands twice, and on the second clap, a huge boulder rolled across the mouth of the cave trapping Pearl, Astro and the foul-smelling sea water, inside the cave. Then, little by little, the power of the water was prizing the floor of the cave apart, forming a large crack in the floor. Pearl stepped around it with her usual grace and poise (despite being under pressure), but there was soon little floor left for her to step on. Astro made one last colossal magic jump in her direction, flicking out a troll sized kick into Pearl's delicate back at the same time. Pearl let out a shriek and dropped into the deep dark cavity, and into the water. She was sinking deeper and deeper into it, her hands crashing around on the surface,

S.E.Aitken

she was trying to swim back to the top, but her efforts were in vain. She was fully immersed in the water now. She decided she must at least take a deep breath and hold it before the water fully consumed her. Astro grasped the fork once more, examining the floor in search of the original fork holes. On finding them, he placed the fork in the same place so that its prongs filled the holes, which in turn stopped the water fountain. He then clapped his hands once more and the cave ground completely closed with Pearl trapped underwater beneath it with no means of escape.

CHAPTER 11

THE SMILING MERMAID

'Ridiculous, what does she think she is doing?' Alex said out loud talking to himself. He tightened the straps on his boots in ready for what he knew would be a long hike. He still could not quite believe that Pearl had been so stubborn to take off without him, especially in a place she was not familiar with. She had been gone only minutes, when he knew he must follow her, but keep a safe distance. He didn't want to upset her by getting too close. He plodded slowly behind, close enough to see her tiny frame, but not close enough to alert her to his presence. She was fiercely independent and would not thank him for the escort. That, coupled with the fact that he had let her down many years ago when they were childhood sweethearts by kissing another girl, which meant the relationship between them as adults had always been a little strained. It was easy to keep up, her tiny strides were no match

147

for the pace his long legs could achieve. They were approximately ten kilometres into the journey, and he could see Pearl was starting to tire. Her steps much shorter now, and her feet dragged on the floor. She had clearly come to a place where she could no longer muster the strength to lift her feet. Alex grimaced as he watched her trip on the occasional stone as a result of her slovenly shuffle. He wished she would take a break, but knew she was determined to keep going until she reached the shore. He was sure, even if they had walked together, she would not have listened had he implored her to rest. Still, that was the Pearl he knew and loved, even if he was not prepared to admit it to her. He was glad when she finally reached the cove and sat down. It was not before time; he was sure if she had tried to walk much further, she would have fell, or feinted. He found a cove close to hers, keeping a watchful eye on her. He a stumbled on a larger rock and sat down on it, which ordinarily it would not have made a comfortable perch, but he was so drained, it felt like the softest feather bed. Too soft in fact, soft enough to lull him into a gentle slumber. He felt his eyes start to drop, so he shuffled on the rock, trying to wake himself. He gave his eyes a vigorous rub at the same time. His eyelids started to droop in defiance at all his attempts to fight sleep. He gently, slapped his own face. *Wake up* he urged his sleepy self, but slowly he began to slide down the rock. Totally energy less and overwhelmed by the urge to sleep. It was not long until he eventually succumbed to it. He remembers his last thought as, *if I close my eyes for just a second, I may feel a little better.* Fortunately, Pearl could not hear the grumble of his snore from where she was resting.

Shortly after, he woke with a start, unsure of how long he had been sleeping. The monkey like sound of a Kookaburras cry bringing him around rather abruptly. He leapt to his feet, chastising himself for sleeping whilst he was on unofficial guard duty. He straightened his armour which had become twisted whilst he slept. Then leaned around the boulder to catch a glimpse of Pearl. She must have moved position he thought because she was no longer in his line of sight. He stepped cautiously around the boulder, trying to stay balanced on a very thin ledge. There was still no sign of Pearl. He decided he must climb down and get a little closer. He stepped down each rock with care, he needed to stay in one piece if he was going to be of any assistance to Pearl should she need him. He reached the sun scorched sand. His boots burying themselves in it with every lunge forward. Not the best footwear for a beach, it was like running through treacle he mused. He came to the quick realisation that Pearl was not here anymore, but where could she be. The beach was empty of obstructions, he could see for miles, if she had headed off, she would still be in view surely? He could see where she had been sitting, there was a Pearl shaped imprint in the sand. This gave him an idea, maybe there were footprints. He checked the floor; all he could see were small claw like feet marks trailing in a Southerly direction. He leaned against a large swaying palm tree which had created a semblance of shade for Pearl earlier in the day.

'Maybe you should try looking into the cave?' He heard a honey sweet female voice say. He revolved around on his heel and could not quite comprehend what he saw. The palm tree had a mouth, and a voice! Alex stepped away from it gingerly. Not wanting to engage in conversation with whatever it was. He didn't understand how it could be talking, was this White or Sable Witch magic. Either way, he was fresh out of ideas on where Pearl could be, and whether the tree was being kind or wicked, it did not seem like a bad idea to check the cave. It did not look to be too far, perhaps she had become too hot and had sought shelter in the cave. He himself had noticed how ruddy and inflamed his skin which was not covered by armour had become since they started their journey. Alex was a little worried that Pearl may have chosen a shelter which was not the haven she may have anticipated. Australia is known for having some of the deadliest creatures in the world, but hopefully, Pearl had enough magical powers to deal with them, but only if she saw them, before they saw her. He trudged up the dunes towards the cave. On reaching it, he called out:

'Hello? Are you in here Pearl?'

Astro crouched in the corner, remaining very still. *Here comes the so-called hero*, he chuckled to himself. *Two for the price of one!* He snorted.

'Pearl, if you are here, let me know, I just need to know you are okay?' Alex cried, one hand placed to the side of his mouth, creating a loudspeaker type effect. A stray stone rolled slowly past his toes, he followed it with a curious gaze until it came to a standstill next to what looked to be a small foot. He raised his eyes higher to find an ugly, grinning troll. He reeled back, taking two steps backwards as he did. Completely surprised and uncomfortable with the appearance of Astro.

'Welcome Alex the White Witch. I have heard so much about you!' He said with a hint of sarcasm. He stretched out his hand, offering a handshake.

Alex did not respond. His uneasy gaze skimming Astro from top to bottom.

'Cannot say the same about you' he mumbled in a weak effort to remain polite, still fervently searching the room for signs of Pearl. The now dry cave floor, not giving away any clues. He walked to each corner of the cave, inspecting its every detail, hoping to find a trace of her. He had started to give up hope, when he noticed the golden fork, standing in full view. A gush of wind circled around him and as it did, something floating on the fork's prongs caught his attention. It was light, floaty, long, and black. He looked more closely, and was mortified when he realised, it was a clump of Pearls hair. When the fork had passed her head, it had caught and removed a bunch of her hair and there it was, the only undeniable evidence that she had been here. He spun on his heel, the hardest masculine glare passing over his face.

'Where is she, what have you done with her?' He demanded to know. He had tugged the hair from the fork and was shaking it in the air at Astro's eye level.

'I know she was here; this is her hair. Tell me where she is right now!' He ordered.

Astro did not feel in the least bit threatened. He looked down bemused, inspecting his dirty fingernails in a nonchalant manner. Alex felt the anger rising in his chest, his breathing started to quicken as his furious heart raged.

'I swear, if you do not tell me where she is, you will wish you had' he growled. He passed his hand teasingly over the tip of the forks handle, raising one threatening eyebrow. Astro remained quiet, safe in the knowledge (or so he thought) that Alex and his puny White Witch magic was no real threat. Then, leaving Astro no time to think, he placed both hands on the fork handle, lugging it free from its standing position in the ground. It seemed effortless compared to Astros previous unsuccessful effort to do the same. He launched the fork using as much of his strength as he could. It flew purposefully through the air. Its path true and unstoppable. As it reached Astro, he swerved to the left. Lifting one gnarled aging hand, he batted it to the floor. It landed with a twang, the sound reverberating across the dismal grey cave walls. Alex resolutely focused on his desire to injure Astro, had not noticed the swirl of sea water rising in the cave, now at knee height. The removal of the fork from the ground had reopened the holes in the ground and water burst its way through them. Astro propelled himself into the air, landing safely on a ledge at least ten feet above Alex. He placed one hand proudly on his hip, and with the other, began to slowly wave.

'Bye, bye Alex, nice knowing you!' He said scathingly. He laughed a deep throaty cackle. Alex felt the water reach his chest causing him to tremble uncontrollably. It was icy cold. His chin quivered, and his teeth clattered together. He was so cold he could not think clearly. How had the cave filled with water he puzzled? Looking to his left, he wondered if he could drag his legs through the force of the water towards the cave entrance. Slowly, he stepped around in a semi-circle, positioning himself so that the cave exit was more visible. Except it was not. Astro had anticipated Alex's next move and clapped his hands causing the giant boulder that had trapped Pearl moments earlier, to roll across the cave exit. Now Alex was a prisoner too, with the water level in the cave rising with every second that passed. It soon reached Alex's chin. It was in that moment that the ground give way with the pressure of the water and began to separate. A large cavity opened beneath their feet, as it did, Alex dropped quickly below the level of the water. He grabbed a last breath, gripped his nose with both fingers and tried to keep his eyes open. The saltwater leaking into them causing them to sting. Alex struggled to keep them open. His only thought being, that he should close them to relieve the painful pressure of the water. He thrashed his arms and legs, writhing his body upwards, trying to reach the surface before he needed the next breath. He thought his lungs would burst until eventually, his efforts paid off. He could see the blurred lighting of the cave through the surface of the water. He raised a hand in the air, trying to push it above water level, and as he did, his hand met a solid object with a thwack. His knuckles ached with the pain of the impact. He raised the other hand. 'Thwack', there it was again. When Alex had dropped into the water, Astro had closed the floor above his head with a clap of his Sable Witch magic and he was trapped. Alex's heart began to pound inside his chest. His lungs could not hold on much longer, they needed air.

Pearl floated weightlessly in the sea, her raven black hair splayed around her face and floating on the curve of the waves. It was like a perfectly orchestrated magazine photo shoot. Except, this photo could have cost Pearl her life. Earth was miles above her, too far to even contemplate a swim for safety. She floated deeper and deeper into the alluring azure blue sea, arms floating out to each side, and her slim legs outstretched in surrender to the seas legendary, unforgiving ways. Her thoughts moved to the Pearl tucked tightly inside her armour. Her trusty Pearl could not even help her now. A combination of sheer exhaustion, and the rocking motion of the sea meant there was no way she would be able to coordinate her arms enough to reach it, and if she could, her brain was so mashed she had no idea how to use it. She was literally, losing the will to live. She cast her mind back to when she first found it. Her mother had been so excited. 'It is yours Pearl, you have found the Freshwater Pearl of Zhejiang' and she remembered that life changing moment so vividly. The combination of her mother's loving embrace and the feeling of total protection as she caressed the Pearl in the palm of her hand. 'Your life will never be the same' she heard her mother say in the chamber of her now fading memories. Never really knowing that it might be such a short life, based on where she found herself now. The only thing she felt grateful for at that very moment was, that she had at least met Alex. She pictured his face for what she thought was the last time. His blond, wispy, shoulder length hair and cobalt blue eyes, flickering with fun and life whenever he looked at her. That look never changed from the moment they first met, it was the look which meant she could never be mad at him for too long, the look that drew her into his company, night after night, fight after fight. The look that she had fell in love with. Even though she was slowly drowning, the sudden realisation that she had always loved Alex seemed scarier than the fact she might die at that very moment. She blinked helplessly, as bubbles of oxygen found their way out of her tightly closed lips. It was time. She needed to take a breath. She opened her lips and, 'crack'. Something had fixed itself over her mouth. She could not see it, but it was stuck across her nose and mouth. It felt hard in texture against her soft skin. A shock of green hair found its way into her peripheral vision, she twisted her head around to find the origin of this mane of green hair and found a striking exquisite looking mermaid. She smiled showing pearl white teeth and warm green eyes. Her eyes almost matching the colour of her hair. She took the object off Pearl's face, and waved it in front of her eyes, then placing it on her own mouth, she showed Pearl what she must do. Pearl could see it more clearly now; it was half an oyster shell, white on the inside and murky grey on the outside. It was incredibly familiar to her. She had seen so many when she was a young girl. It was just like the shell she found her own Pearl inside, all those years ago. The strangest thing is, as soon as the shell reached her mouth, she was able to breathe freely. She gave a quiet thank you, even though she knew the mermaid probably could not hear her through the shell and the noise of the seas current. Then she considered, perhaps mermaids could not hear at all? She would never have believed they existed had she not been looking right at one. The mermaid never dropped her smile, it was so very welcoming. Pearl instinctively felt safe. She took Pearl's hand and began to navigate her deep into the ocean. Pearl took deep breaths of clean pure air from the shell. She kicked her feet in the hope that this would make the journey to wherever the mermaid was taking her much swifter. It felt like only minutes before she could see a large structure ahead of them in the water. As they swam closer, she could see it was an enormous glittering Oyster shell. It was bigger than Queen Diamond's palace which was a phenomenal structure. They were almost on top of it when the mermaid paused. Her green shimmering tail gently swishing from side to side. She glanced at Pearl, pointing at her own mouth, as if to say, copy me. She yawned the biggest yawn, then pointed to Pearl. Pearl took the shell from her mouth and forced herself to yawn, doing her best not to drink in any sea water. She slammed the shell back to her mouth to regain breath. On both yawns, the sound of random musical chords echoed through the air and the giant clam began to judder open. The mermaid gestured to Pearl that they must go in, Pearls eyes widened in awe at what she saw inside the shell. It was a stunning crystal palace, shimmering through the veil of the sea water. She had never seen anything quite so beautiful. The smiling mermaid blew her a gentle kiss and kicked her tail into the air. She gave a twirl, then disappeared towards the mouth of the oyster. She gave a large yawn revealing the Pearl coloured tonsils that only mermaids usually had. The same tonsils which granted access to the Clam Palace. Unbeknown to Pearl, she had the very same tonsils, and this very fact, made her one of the mermaid family.

♭♭♭

Alex floated lifeless in the water. He had long lost the ability to hold his breath. He lay face down and motionless. The smiling mermaid wasted no time. She clamped the clam shell onto his face in the hope that it was not too late. He was remarkably heavy, but she managed to slowly haul him through the water, the same way as she had Pearl. The journey to Clam Palace took considerably longer this time. Her mermaid arms ached with Alex's weight, but she made a heroic struggle to get him to safety. After what seemed like an age to her, she reached the Clam. She gave a wide yawn and the Clam partially opened. A fierce looking bearded merman came to the entrance.

'What is this, this thing has not been granted access. Does he have Pearl tonsils?'

The smiling mermaid dropped her smile for the first time.

'Step back Ludwig, this is White Witch Pearls companion. If we do not get him to safety, he may not survive' The merman nodded sternly.

'Very well, permission to enter granted' he announced, hitting a large glowing red button at the side of the clam entrance.

They lay Alex on the ground on a bed of glowing crystals. Pearl rushed to his side when she saw him arrive.

'What happened, is he going to be okay?' She asked anxiously.

The mermaid gave a gentle nod as she gestured to the jelly fish to join them. The jelly fish hovered above his still lifeless body and began to pass their legs across each part of his body. Pearl shook her head in disbelief. They were going to brush Alex with jelly fish, was she dreaming. It felt too surreal to be true. Suddenly a line of clear transparent jelly fish floated in, and as she had predicted they began to rise and fall in a line above Alex, each time they dropped they made contact with the unconscious Alex. Each time they did, a spark of light appeared in the place their legs touched.

'Does that hurt him? Don't those things sting. I am really not comfortable with this!' Pearl said hurriedly.

Relax Pearl, they only sting things that are threatening them. They also have healing powers. They are Moon Jelly fish, and as such, they carry magical healing powers which they absorb from the moon. That is the only reason they move around in the sea. They are recharging in the light of the moon. Pearl gulped and shuffled her feet in the space she was standing, she could not see the mermaid speak, but it was as though the answers came into her head telepathically. Her hands were now firmly crossed across her chest. She wore a silver blanket one of the sea horses had provided her when she first arrived. Ten minutes passed and there appeared to be no change from Alex. Pearl had begun to pace the room like an expectant Father. *Why was this taking so long* she thought? Her anxiety was reaching new highs and she was compelled by a need to do something. She pushed past one of the jelly fish's legs which were dangling at eye level in front of her face. She brushed it away in that no nonsense Pearl style she is renowned for. She began to speak to Alex.

'Alex, Alex its Pearl, are you there. I need you to come back to me. If you do not come back to me, you will be in serious trouble. I mean it!' The jelly fish had floated backwards now, pausing to allow Pearl to get closer. Alex did not respond. He lay lifeless, his arms limp at either side of the multi-coloured space age looking crystal table. The smiling mermaid nodded her head at the jelly fish, gesturing that they should leave the area and give Pearl and Alex a moment.

'Alex, please don't leave me. I just could not face life without you and…. Well…. I know I am not always kind to you, but, well, I do love you. Please Alex, PLEASE. Don't quit on me now' She rested her head on his chest, not applying too much pressure. She did not want to add to his delicate condition. The tears began to flow down her cheeks. She pushed her face into his chest to smother the sound of her uncontrollable sobbing. She could not believe she might never hear his voice again. A few moments passed until she felt a hand stroking her hair.

'Pearl, I never knew you felt that way. I thought you hated me. Pearl I love …' Pearl jerked quickly upright on the sound of Alex's voice. She looked cross. She felt as though she had been tricked into revealing her true feelings.

'Don't you ever do that to me again' she scolded.

'I mean what are you even doing here. Were you following me or something?' She paced the room, stroking her fingers through her hair in a perplexed manner.

Alex raised his eyebrows and screwed up his eyes in confusion. He looked at the smiling mermaid, and then to Pearl. The mermaid gave an understanding supportive shrug. Alex took Pearl's hand, in his and pulled her chin in the direction of his gaze.

'Pearl, I came back, where did YOU go, what happened to your nice words?' Pearl avoided his gaze embarrassed with her earlier display of affection. She played with her hair, trying to decide if she was prepared to continue with the conversation, but before she made her decision, her thoughts were interrupted with an earth-shattering bang. The clam shook and quaked, scattering the crystal furniture in all directions. The jelly fish slapped to the wall and the mermaids landed on top of them. The jelly fish managed to unsucker themselves from the crystal walls of the palace, their tiny eyes cross eyed from the crushing mermaid body slams. The mermaids slowly slithered to the glass type floor and were sliding uncontrollably across it. Alex and Pearl were locked in an accidental clinch with the force of the tremor. Pearl still refusing to make eye contact with Alex. Then the aggressive looking merman gate keeper Ludwig scrambled back into the room.

'I have locked the hatches; it is Astro the troll. He is outside firing bolts of fire at the clam entrance' Ludwig received no response, everything and everyone in the room were focused on staying on their feet and tails through the smashing and thumping vibrations.

Astro had discreetly followed Alex into the depths of the ocean. Staying at a distance where Alex had no inkling of his presence around him. Astro did not want to take any chances. He needed to make sure Alex and Pearl did not get remotely close to finding Lucas Cave. He could not imagine the shame if he were the only Sable Witch servant who failed in his mission. Trolls hated water and he was no exception. At first, he spluttered and coughed as he entered the water, shortly before abandoning the thought of attempting to swim. He was not equipped for the athleticism that this would involve. His little legs and arms wriggling at full speed, in a hilarious attempt to at least move in the water. Instead, he held his hands at shoulder height, palms facing away from his body, and began to chant that eerie, gobbledegook he had spoken back in the cave. His voice growing louder and shriller. It was Astro's least favourite spell, the noise and decibels it needed to make it happen always gave him a whopping headache. Needs must, he thought, battling his way through the blare. Minutes later, there was a sharp flash of light and he found he was floating effortlessly through the water. He reached out in front of him to confirm his spell had worked. His hand met an iridescent force field around him. He was floating in a totally transparent, air filled, bubble. Water could not touch him. The only thing he needed to do, was to push the bubble force field in the direction of Alex, like a hamster would push a wheel. He was proud of his cunning plan. He now had a clear unhindered view of Alex and the mermaid directly ahead and sneakily hovered in the background. The only mistake in his plan was the distance he had created between them. It was so great; he was unable to gain enough speed to clear the entrance of the Clam Palace at the same time as they did. Alex and the mermaid. It had closed before he was able to reach it. He cracked his hand against the clam wall in frustration, sending a sharp pain which started in his fist then travelled up his arm. He sat cross legged now, his force field bubble bobbing up and down on the path of the water. He needed a new plan, and fast. *I must gain access to the Clam, but how*, he contemplated. The answer came to him out of the blue. Of course, he should use the strongest power the Sable Witches had in their repertoire, send balls of fire to the clam gate. *Why didn't I think of this before* he laughed? The only minor obstacle was that he would need to release the force field to send the fire balls from his hand to the clam. He sighed resigned to the fact that another migraine was on its way. He would have to complete the magical chant to reinstate it. Once he had finished. He launched the fireballs at the clam walls with all his strength, powered by a horrible desire to crumble the clam's protective hard-shell exterior. One after the other, the fireballs crashed into the shell, sending enormous shock waves through it, to the point that the whole shell visibly shook, but the clam lid remained stubbornly closed. The clam had lived on the seabed for hundreds of years, surviving battle after battle. Astro's magic was no match for the clam. Hearing all of the commotion through the waves of the water, a gang of octopuses had begun to crowd around the clam walls. They began to fire ink at Astro, squirt after squirt the thick black ink had almost covered him entirely. It started to seep into the corners of his mouth. He repeatedly tried to wipe it away, but it was landing on him thick and fast, he looked down at the mess he had got himself into, dripping with black octopi's ink and, still no closer to gaining entry to the Clam. Astro blazed with anger, his cheeks inflamed with the rise in his heart rate and blood pressure.

'Okay, that is it!' He said in temper

'If you won't let me in. I won't let you out!' He screamed, before launching into his unearthly deafening magical chant. This time his chant more powerful than the last. The rise in his temper had caused a surge in his magical powers, and with the flick of his wrists once more, the Clam Palace became trapped in a giant force field.

'Now, nobody can get in and nobody can get out!' Sneered Astro. Brushing his hands together in a dusting motion, he sat in his own force field bubble of evil, totally content that his mission had been successful.

CHAPTER 12

THE MESSAGE FROM EMERALD

Daylin walked quietly over to his bedroom window. The floorboards sometimes creaked, and he did not want to wake anyone. He felt the need to take a long look through his bedroom window. It had been a long time since he had seen his room, or the village, life seemed so much simpler in those days. Little Love Forest always had a calming, quiet serenity about it at night. After recent events, serenity is just what he needed. He pulled back the shabby curtains that Father had never replaced them since Mum passed away. He could not bring himself to change anything about the house. Almost like he expected her to arrive home at any minute and complain that things were not as she left them. He opened the rickety wooden window, desperately in need of a lick of paint, but again, that would mean changing the colour, and father had been reluctant to do that to. He would need to do that for him when he returned. He drew in the night air, a familiar mix of fresh chopped wood and wildflowers flushed through his nostrils. There were always piles of wood neatly stacked around the house, freshly prepared by his father, waiting on the villagers to come and collect them. He looked up at the blanket of dazzling stars winking back at him in the night sky. His heart gave a sneeze like flutter. He so loved the stars, and he could always get a clear view of them from his room. He was about to close the window and turn around when he saw a change in the star arrangement. It was the strangest thing. The stars seemed to move and reassemble themselves in some kind of pattern. He had never seen anything like it but was sure there was magic at work. Nothing surprised him these days. The more time he spent with the White Witches, the more he became accustomed to unusual occurrences. He looked to his right and saw Sapphire leaning out of his father's window, brushing her hair.

'It's not good news I am afraid' She whispered staring straight ahead at the array of stars in the sky. Of course, she knew Daylin was there. Sapphire was incredibly wise.

'It is a message from Emerald, she says the Sable Witches have been mischievous. They have swapped Lightning Pass with Thunder Pass. The others have already been tricked into travelling through it'

'What, are they okay?' He asked, not sure how she could still be so calm in such circumstances.

'Not sure, hopefully they have been able to look after themselves. It is a dark and sinister place. All I know now is, we must not take it. Emerald says we can only get to Australia by flying on Nodrog again. It is the safest way.' Daylin nodded solemnly, now completely consumed with concern about Ruby's welfare. His imagination sending the scariest images of her racing through his mind. He could not speak and was unwilling to share his thoughts with Sapphire, not wanting to alarm her. He whispered

'Goodnight' and gently closed the window.

Sapphire was first to wake and had begun toasting bread on the roaring fire. The bakery like smell finding its way under Daylin's bedroom door and creeping into Duke's nostrils as he snored loudly on the sofa. Nodrog's eyes were also closed, and his chin brushed the cabin floor whilst sleeping. He wore the same cheerful smile even whilst he was at rest. The smell of toast bringing him out of his doze. He picked up his head sniffing in the general direction of the toast and in doing so, cracked his head on the roof of the cabin. The cabin rocked with the impact awakening Duke and Daylin at the same time. Daylin dashed out of the bedroom ready to take on the world. Duke sat up and raised his hand in the air.

'Don't panic, it was just Nodrog forgetting where he was. I think his head took quite a bash on the ceiling poor thing' Nodrog let out a gentle sigh and rolled his eyes to the heavens. Duke, Sapphire and Daylin chuckled sympathetically each one taking their turn to give his head a healing stroke.

Daylin finished the hot tea he had been swilling around in his Father's favourite 'Don't Panic, I am a Wood Cutter' mug. There was no sweeter tea than that you find in Little Love Forest. It was the combination of its distinctive heart-warming taste, and the fact that Daylin wanted to spend a few more minutes with his Father, that had made him take so long to drink it. Sapphire sensed his reluctance and took charge.

'Okay, it will not be long until we see you again Duke. Thank you so much for your hospitality. It was truly lovely to meet you!'

Duke wiped the remnants of butter from his hand. He had not washed them since assisting Sapphire with the toast a short time earlier, they made quite the choreographed domestic couple. It was nice to have the company of a lady in the cabin. It had been a long time. He extended his buttery hand to Sapphire with a gracious smile. Sapphire frowned, throwing both hands around his neck in a caring squeeze. She had grown very fond of Duke in the short time they had spent in his home, and vice versa. Duke blushed a little.

'Lovely to meet you too Sapphire, please come and visit, any time you like?' He suggested.

'And me?' Daylin joked.

'Of course, my beautiful boy, you are always welcome home!'

Nodrog, sniffed the rug next to the fire, oblivious of the conversation, or what was coming next. Daylin caressed his head once more.

'I hate to disturb you my friend, but we need your services again. Do you think you could get us safely to Lucas Cave in Australia?' He did not want to share any other detail than this. Nodrog had done such a sterling job of getting everyone to (what they thought was) Lightening Pass, he did not want him to think he had brought any trouble to his friends the White Witches. Nodrog gave that wide ear to ear grin. Happy to be part of the rescue committee once more. He twisted his neck back and two in the window in which it was jammed, until it released with a pop. He was back outside and beaming a wide toothy grin, ready for the next adventure.

CHAPTER 13

MERCY FOR THE MUMMY

The Mummy threw himself into Thunder Pass, already impatient at the time it took to get there. Impatience was one of the most notable aspects of his character, alongside his general grumpiness. He had no time for the 'Unstable Sables' (as he quietly referred to them inwardly), much less their employees. He always seemed to get tangled up with their dirty schemes and he was tiring of it. He had an absolute distain for being their puppet but was a prisoner to this life. His powers were far inferior to that of the Sable Witches. If he rose against them, he would not win, and he had always known it. The Sable Witches had captured him and his family and would only release them if they all agreed to become Mummy servants of the Sable Witch realm. It was a sad but true story. Since that time, being the youngest and the fittest family member, he was always sent on missions against the White Witches. The same

White Witches that used to be his friend. It took all his resolve to do as they asked, but he could not live with the consequences if he didn't. He loved his family so much, he needed to get to his destination, do the terrible deed. Then return to his family. Every minute he was away from them, he worried what heinous acts the Sable Witches might inflict on them. He never trusted them at their word. Just because he was being compliant, never meant they were truly safe. The Sable Witches could not be trusted, not even amongst themselves.

'Take your hands off me' he demanded. Snarling at the shadows as they reached out pawing his bandages.

'I am one of the Sable Witches servants too, now leave me alone and let me pass!' He screamed.

This was exactly as he knew it would be. There was no allegiance in the Sable Witch community. You were completely on your own. Every man and woman for themselves. Each time a stray shadow hand came towards him he showed a yellow set of teeth and snapped away at them. Hoping this would be enough of deterrent. The shadows were not deterred. The Mummy's teeth could not penetrate their ghost like arms. This only encouraged them even more. They began to prod him with their bony fingers, this way and that. Mummy tried to swim through more quickly now, thrusting his arms backwards and forwards in a breaststroke action. Trying to propel himself further forward in the hope that this would accelerate his journey up. He neared the pass exit when the shadows decided they would have one last play with him. They grabbed at his arms and pulled him backwards back into the cave. Then fired him forward like a cannon ball back towards the exit from where he came. Mummy could hear the whistling of the wind as he raced towards the exit. He travelled at high speed, his ears popping with the turbulent wind in the pass.

Then, moments later, thud, he landed at the mouth of Thunder Pass, Validor side.

'Where too?' Asked a rough male voice.

Mummy strained his neck to see who was talking to him. There was a stagecoach parked close by and a bald man in a checked waist coat, smoking a pipe filled with Pink tobacco stood casually at the entrance of Thunder Pass. Mummy let out a moan, winded by the high impact of landing on a solid cobble stoned path.

'Speak up lad, where do you want to go. I can't wait all night' the voice spoke again. Mummy puzzled at the statement. Validor was in total darkness now, even in daytime.

'I, I need to get to the White Witch coven' he struggled, still hurting from his torpedo style flight.

'Oh yeah, what do you want with the Coven lad?' Replied the coach driver in a curious voice which carried a hint of cautiousness.

'Ask no questions and you won't get hurt' sneered the Mummy. Starting to remember his role in this. He needed to look strong and forceful. The driver tapped his pipe on the floor to empty the spent tobacco onto the floor. Not in the least threatened by the Mummy. He had seen far worse in his lifetime.

'Come on then, in you get. On your head be it' he warned.

The coach rattled into life and the horses began a slow trot, picking up the pace with each second before reaching a full canter. Mummy looked out of the dirty glass window; he could see nothing amidst the backdrop of a black foreboding sky. His stomach turned with the motion and lack of visibility, but the speed worked for him. *The sooner the better* he thought. Thirty minutes or so had passed when he felt the coach begin to reduce speed. Slowly but surely, it ground to a halt. He waited for a moment, half expecting the coach driver to stick his head through the window and at least explain why they had stopped. There was nothing, no sign of him. He wrenched open the door of the carriage and dropped his feet onto the cobble stones. His legs seemingly protesting with a sharp stabbing pain in complaint of their motionless journey.

'What is going on, why have we stopped?' he asked frostily.

'Pumpkin strike, they want more pay see. They won't let us pass' he said coolly, holding a lighted match to his pink tobacco filled pipe. He sat comfortably, anticipating a long wait until the Pumpkins eventually dispersed.

'Seriously?' The Mummy responded, snatching the pipe from the coach driver, and throwing it to the floor. The coach driver did not react.

'Yep, if you need to get to the Coven sooner, you will have to walk. It is not that far now'. He drew a ripped newspaper page from his pocket, unfolding it on his lap. He took out an eye glass from his waist coat pocket and started to read with it. The Mummy could not believe what he was hearing and seeing, he was furious at the driver's complacent attitude. He walked towards the group of chunnering pumpkins and began kicking them one by one. Launching them into the air one after the other. They flew high in the air like giant orange medicine balls. Mummy started to feel a little better, he felt less angry with every strike of his foot into each plump pumpkin bauble. Every time one came to be in his path, his kick became more forceful, catapulting them uncaringly through the air.

'OY, OY, Stop that!' The coach driver interjected. The Mummy turned to face him, then gave him a hard shove, sending him reeling into the bushes close by. He could not waste time on petty demonstrations. He needed to do the wicked Sable Witch deed, then get back to his family as quickly as was feasible. He had no time to lose. He ploughed on taking impressive purposeful strides towards the White Witch Coven Castle gate.

Emerald carefully brushed the nail polish across her toenails with the expertise of a fully trained beautician. This was her weekly ritual; she had been doing this for as long as she could remember. Albeit things were a little different this evening. This time, she was painting by candlelight. A dainty pale foot propped on a velvet tasseled cushion, she leant across her outstretched leg, gliding the brush against each perfectly pedicured toe. As you might imagine. This was no ordinary nail polish. As soon as a drop met her toenail, it formed photograph like images of each White Witch. She could have chosen any picture she liked, but she missed her family so much. So, her White Witch family were today's choice. This helped with the worry and loneliness. Often, she would add nail photographs of pretty garden flowers, or brilliant planets, but not today. She placed the brush back in the pot tightening the lid, satisfied with her own little toe tribute. Just as she had begun to congratulate herself on a job well done, she heard the familiar hoot of her Owls at the Palace gate. It was a shrill unusual hoot she knew it to be the intruder alert, somebody or something was attempting to get into the palace. Emerald kept remarkably still. Unsure of what to do next. After all, she was on her own and did not know what she might meet if she tried to confront whatever it might be. She tried to tune into the minds of the owls at the gate. Mind reading owls was particularly difficult and the results not always clear. She trod into the virtual corridor of owl Kikazarus mind, connecting to his vision first. He seemed to be perched up high, on the very top of one of the Castle turrets. She looked down with him and saw a figure wrapped in bandages standing still in front of the rippling gate force field. The figure tipped his head from one side to the other, as if he were trying to make sense of what he was seeing. The force field shining in the light of the night, all colours of the rainbow. He lifted one arm and poked a tightly bandaged finger into the force field. A shock of electricity passed through him, in the same colours as the force field and tossed him backwards. He began to roll uncontrollably down the castle path, completing head spinning flipping and twirling that even the best gymnast in the world might not attempt. Emerald gave a shrewd smile. The force field gate had been designed to do this. It had not been tested too often, but she was glad that tonight of all nights, it was on form. She disengaged from Kikazarus mind and furiously pulled on her satin slippers. Queen Diamond's guards had heard the commotion and were crashing through the corridors in full armor towards the palace gate. Mummy managed to scramble back onto his feet a little dazed from his shock. His arm and leg bandages flapping loosely around his person. He heard a stomping sound from behind. It seemed to be increasing in decibels. He saw nothing except the black cloak of the night, disguising everything except the Palace gate. He stumbled around flummoxed that his bandages had started to unravel. He grabbed one or two pieces and tried to roll it back around his arms and legs. It was not the best look, but the bandages had served to protect him in the past from some of his darkest enemies and of course they disguised who he really was. The bandages were of no use, too torn and ragged to use again. When he had tried correcting his bandages, he had not noticed that quite a crowd had gathered behind him. He heard a cough so turned round to face it. Close to his feet were hundreds of battered and irate Pumpkins. Some of them wearing the imprint of his big, clubbed bandage feet having kicked them minutes earlier. One of them gave a loud shout.

S.E.Aitken

'Get him!' He instructed the others. Instantaneously, the pumpkins took it in turns to roll heavily across the mummy's feet. Mummy hopped around like a demented frog, trying to avoid each one with his feet, it was impossible, there were too many. His feet started to throb and swell within his bandages, causing them to tighten and smart. He had nowhere to go, and his feet started to cut and blister. When he could stand no more, he fell to the floor and once again the pumpkins started to perform their relentless dance, now having full access to his entire body. They began to pound it without mercy. The guards burst through the palace force field and could not believe what they had walked into. They had never seen so many pumpkins in one space. They stood still in wonder at the scene in front of their very eyes. There was little they needed to do; the pumpkins seemed to have this under control. They leant against the wall, arms folded, whispering to one another and pointing at some of the crazy pumpkin antics unfolding before them. The coach driver caught up with the Pumpkins now. He walked calmly over to one of the palace guards.

'I tried to warn him. Nasty piece of work though. Deserves all he gets I say' Once again he removed his favourite pipe from his waist coat and lit it, joining the guards propped against the wall, he continued to look on as though it was a favourite TV show that he had missed last week. Emerald had forgotten how many steps there were in the Castle. There had been no need in recent days for her to try to move from one room to the next. It was quite a marathon chasing her way behind the Queens guard to the gate. She never noticed the distance before, but this time she puffed and panted her way through it. Not the usual composed Emerald everyone was used to. Eventually she pushed through the force field into the crazed pumpkin soup. She tentatively stepped around them, not wanting her new nail polish to be chipped by any unintentional or intentional bashing against a pumpkin.

172

'What on earth is going on?' She inquired, searching the faces of a guard close to stone arch of the gate.

'Pumpkin war, it seems this mummy attacked some of them earlier and now they really mad' There were so many bounding orange pumpkins that the mummy was covered with them. Emerald stepped across one or two, trying to make out if the mummy was still amongst them. As she got further into the pile, she could just make out a head and two eyes peeping through a set of rapidly unravelling bandages. As the bandages unraveled, she could see more and more of what was beneath them. It was a human, a young scared looking male. He looked at her tears streaming down his face but was in too much pain to talk. As their eyes connected, she found herself travelling into his mind. She saw a human family, playing in a corn field, two children and a woman who looked to be their mother. Although they looked reasonably content, they were surrounding by dark shadows with red piercing eyes. They were captives, all of them. Emerald realized she had climbed into a recent memory. She looked to the doorway of the cottage through his mind's eye, and there stood a man, looking devotedly at his family. She managed to zoom in on his face. Yes, she was sure it was the same blue eyes she saw bloodshot and tearful right in front of her. It was then she understood this man was a Sable Witch prisoner, as was his family. He had no choice but to do what he had been asked to do. A wave of sympathy swept over her. She pushed back through the pumpkins and started to climb the whitewashed castle walls, until she could see the whole army of pumpkins beneath her.

'STOP, STOP RIGHT NOW!' She bawled.

The pumpkins continued their uncoordinated mummy bashing activities. The guards jumped to attention. Emerald was their Queen since Queen Diamond was no longer with them, and they had vowed to treat her as such. At least until a new Queen was found. They leapt into battle, using their spears to knock the pumpkins away from the Mummy, one by one. They did this lightly and softly. The pumpkins were their friends, and typically they were such passive, non-aggressive beings. Something had certainly got them rattled, and they did not want to stoke the fire. Eventually the pumpkins took the hint, and began to roll away, creating a distance of a few inches between themselves and the injured Mummy.

'This man is innocent; his family are held prisoner by the Sable Witches. He had no choice but to try to fulfil their wishes' she yelled, at the same time as scrambling back down the castle wall. The pumpkins began to roll away sheepishly, leaving Emerald to a moaning and bruised mummy. She dropped to her knees at his side.

'Take him inside please' she asked the guards. They stepped forward without question, lifting the mummy high above their heads. Then marched towards the castle gate. Owl Kikazarus released the force field so they could tramp the mummy inside the castle walls, without causing him any more harm. Then, Kikazarus immediately returned it to its former buzzing glory. They did not need any more surprise guests this evening. Emerald lead them to the Queens bedroom. The other rooms should remain free in case her White Witch family should return early, and unannounced. The site of a mummy in their room may be not the type of greeting they were hoping for. The guards carefully placed a sobbing Mummy onto the bed. Then they dispersed through the bedroom door, back to guard the palace. Emerald trundled into the brilliant white porcelain bathroom, fit for a Queen. She collected towels, cotton wool and warm clean water. She tore the cotton wool, dipping each piece methodically into the white bowl she had retrieved from one of the vanity units in the bathroom. She passed the warm soothing cotton wool across Mummy's face. As she did, his sobbing started to quieten. Swipe after swipe of soft cotton on his skin. She had cleaned all the dirt and stones from his face and hands without uttering a word. Mummy slowly drifted off to sleep. Emerald gave a sympathetic smile. She could not believe what this man had been driven to. Every piece of her being wanted to help him and his family.

'It is going to be okay' she whispered in his ear in a reassuring way.

'When all of this is over, I promise, I will send a message to my friends and ask them to find your family and help them. First you must rest.'

She placed down the bowl at the side of the bed and drew a glass of water. She placed it close to his bed in case he should wake, but there was one more thing she needed to do. She once again, focused on his face, and began to virtually step into his exhausted mind.

'When you wake up, you should not panic, you and your family will be safe. So long as, you will not harm anyone in this palace. Do you promise?' Her words echoed in his head but could not be heard in the bedroom. He gave a slow nod, followed by a long exhale, smacking his lips together, deep in sleep.

'Yes, thank you. I promise' he muttered, still breathing heavily in between his words. She lifted the bowl and cotton wool and carried it back into the bathroom and began to clean up. Queen Diamond may not be here, but her bathroom and room should be left as it was when she was with them. She returned to Mummy to check on him. The bandages still trailed on the floor from beneath the bedclothes she had rested upon him. She started to drag them gently away, one after the other without disturbing either the bedclothes or Mummy. When she was sure she had removed them all, she gathered them into a small bundle and placed them into a white bin sitting next to the large, balcony bay window. She unlocked the balcony door with the silver key still sitting in the lock where Queen Diamond had left it. Stepping out onto the cold marble floor she looked to the stars. Reaching into her pocket she clutched her Emerald, and lifting it high above her head, started to write the story of the Mummy and his family in the sky. Hoping her White Witch family knew how to help.

CHAPTER 14

WHEN THE THREE SISTERS, MET THE THREE SISTERS

The three sisters clumsily stumbled around stupefied by the magic of the Amber. All of them equally transformed into a hypnotic state. None of them with the magical capability to overpower its magic. One by one, they each began to walk the forest trail, completely zombified. They must have been walking aimlessly for at least ten miles, before Amber's spell started to wear off. Unbeknown to them, the spell would only remain with them for as long as they were within a ten-mile radius. They did not quite understand it, they only knew they had wandered deep into the forest of Braeriach, without any clear direction of where they were going. They stopped in the same slot simultaneously standing side by side underneath the shade of the trees, looking equally baffled. Touching their own faces, hands, and legs as if checking they really existed. They then began making their strange ghost like echoey sounds amongst them, speaking their very own three sister's language, a language that could never be translated by anyone but themselves. Then joining together their long boney fingers, they started to skip in a circle, first they start slowly, then increase the tempo with each step. The magic began to rise through them, starting at their toes, and travelling up to their pretty heads full of blond curls. The light of the magic shining through them as it connected with each part of their petite frames. They were immersed in their own magical beacon of light, illuminating the forest like a ships search light. Their magic converged hurtling them into the air like three human rockets, travelling at the speed of light, creeping ever closer to their target Lucas Cave Australia. It was not long until they were there, it was, immediately ahead of them. The smallest of the three sisters gave a shrill, excitable squeal of delight and separated from the others, with a sharp angular change in direction. Separating from the group, she plummeted downwards. The others raised their eyebrows. They were very familiar with their little sisters' impulsive ways and had come to expect it from her. All they could do was reluctantly follow. They had an unspoken sisterly understanding; they must never be separated. If one moves, the others must go too. The youngest mischievously nosedived at great speed towards the floor. Goading the others to follow suit in a game of chicken. Their descent was like a shooting star from the heavens to the ground. Making their eventual landing far less gracious than their take off. Suddenly, all three of them came crashing to the floor, a mash of three ghostly figurines. The smallest jumped to her feet, rushing ahead into the balmy dusk air. Once again, the others sighed, slowly dragging themselves over to the same place she had headed. They found this game a little tiresome, but they forgave her, she was a bundle of fun, always looking for the next adventure. Her intentions were harmless, (to each other at least). She paused at the mountain top leaning against a bulky stone with jagged edges, it was almost as big as her, and a similar shape. There was another joined to it, and then another. The sisters could not quite believe their eyes, it seemed as though it was three gigantic stone versions of the sisters, perched proudly on the mountain top like they had been there for thousands of years. The sisters gaggled in excitement, stroking the stones like they were long lost members of the family. They began talking to them incessantly, hoping for a reaction from the beautiful stone figurines. Brushing themselves against each one like contented cats rubbing and marking their territory. One of the sisters, removed a phone from her pocket and began taking pictures of herself with each statue. The largest of the three took the phone away and through it into the bushes, leaving a very dejected looking sister. They were so taken by the appearance of the three sisters made from rock; they had not noticed someone else had joined them and was lurking quietly in the shadows. Quietly creeping around unnoticed from tree to tree. There was a cough, then a voice said.

'It is the three sisters. The story goes, someone turned them to stone. Probably using similar magic to that you used on Opal?' Said the voice in a matter-of-fact way.

The three sisters craned their neck to see who was speaking to them from behind the whispering trees.

Ruby was feeling pleased with herself. She had resourcefully found her way back through the earth's core and managed to trek as far as Echo Point, Katoomba, finding herself face to face with the famous Blue Mountain three sisters (the craggy mountain side images) and the other three sisters from the Sable Witch realm.

The sisters began to warble in their usual sneaky, weird and unsettling way. Their attentions suddenly switching from the three sisters of stone to their new guest, Ruby. The noises the sisters were making became more protracted, echoing across the landscape around them. It made the hairs on Ruby's head stand up. It was then she realized, this is a sound she had heard once before. It was the same chants which precluded the magic the sisters had bestowed on Opal immediately before she turned into an ice statue. She knew she must react quickly, her heartbeat raising in ready. They had already lost Opal. She needed to make sure their magic did not reach her. She started to frantically search for her Ruby in the pocket of the jeans. Her heart began to sprint around her chest with anxiety. She knew she must use the Ruby somehow. She was terrified she might become the fourth petrified sister at Echo Point. She had no clue of how to stop their magic, but she knew she must try and just as they started to reach that all familiar animated crescendo of noise, she first saw in her Mothers garden. She clasped the Ruby and lifted it from her pocket, pressing it firmly against her clammy forehead.

'Er, Er…How does this thing work' she puzzled out loud. *I just need to get to Lucas Mountain without the three sisters trying to stop me, but how?* She still had no clue how to use the magic of the Ruby. She was so new to White Witch magic, quite the novice, but something deep within her urged her to try. She took the stone away from her head momentarily, so she could think a little. She turned around to see if all three sisters were in the same place, the noise seemed to die down somewhat to a distant drone. As she tried to face them, she realized, they had disappeared. It was as though they had never been there. *Have I been imagining* this she contemplated? She looked back to her Ruby as if expecting it to answer. It was then she dropped the Ruby to the floor in shock, because she could see clearly within the Rubies deep red contours, the miniature images of the three sisters, trapped inside her own precious Ruby. They were moving around and knocking on the walls of the Ruby, their mouths gaping open, as if they were howling and wailing.

Scratching their hands through the air, showing their long, slender, silver clad nails. *Were they trying to scratch their way out?* Ruby questioned; she was not going to waste any time waiting to see if they were successful. Perhaps the Ruby had read her mind and her wish? She did not know or have the time to comprehend. Nor did she know how long she could hold the seething sister's prisoner in her Ruby. All she knew, is that she must leave, and leave now. She needed to make her way to Lucas cave. Ruby knelt to retrieve the Ruby from the floor, grabbing it quickly as if her life depended on it. She crushed it fervently to her forehead, praying that she could telepathically urge it to lead her safely to Lucas Cave. She crammed the Ruby back in her jean pocket and began to run like the wind, weaving in and out of the ancient tree trunks, gliding lightly on her feet in a rhythmic and angelic way. She continually reached into her emotions, using them as a compass to guide the way. Each turn she took, reaching back into her stomach as if asking her instincts to feel if this is the right direction. The long, lush grass passed across her calves with every step, sending soothing strokes of encouragement through to them. She ran down the mountain side like a racing snake, dropping down and down. Panting her way through the dusty heat whilst remaining totally fixated on reaching the cave. She kicked her feet faster. Her once white trousers, now grubby with dirt and sand that had attached itself to her legs. Her breathing became shallow as her energy reserves reached zero. It was time to stop. She leant forward, puffing, and craving a drink. The forest was still except for the gentle swishing of the leaves around her head, the breeze causing them to rattle and shake against each other. She reached out leaning one hand against a thick dry tree trunk. She could smell the earthy musky smell of wood that had weathered a thousand years. She wondered what the trees had seen in their long lifetime. If only they could talk, they would have a story to tell, she was sure. Resisting the desire to be seated, she propped her whole-body weight against the tree.

She was sure if she sat, she might fall asleep. Slowly her breathing returned to a steady, normal pace. She could hear a little more now that her hearing was no longer distorted by her loud gasps for air. Birds circled high in the sky, letting out high pitched calls to one another, and through their chatter, she could make out another familiar and reassuring noise, it was the sound of a babbling brook, or some such thing. It was definitely water running across rock, and not too far away by all accounts. It was close enough for her to just pick up its soft rippling gurgle. Ruby pushed away from the tree and stood high on her tip toes, one hand shadowing her eyes from the sun bursting through the tree canopy. She looked left to right, desperately trying to locate the source of the noise. She was so thirsty; she needed to find the water and take a drink. Her mouth was parched to the point that there was a notable dry white crust forming around her ruby red lips. Her efforts failed. She could not locate the noise. She scuffed the floor in a frustrated protest. As she did, she remembered, she must let her emotions guide her, not her sight. She drew a deep meditative breath. Closed her eyes, then slowly reopened them taking small steps to the left of the tree. As she did, she felt a pang of anxiety bringing her to a sharp stop. She then hesitantly, glided to the right. As she did, she felt a calmness pass through her. Go right, she nodded as if responding to a psychic message from within. She carried on to the right and sure enough, the sound of running water increased. She knew she must be awfully close. It's tinkling and splashing dominating the shrill shriek of the birds.

🎎🎎🎎

Ruby summoned up the energy to keep moving, following the soothing trickling sound of the water, she used her inner compass to guide her towards the caves. Each step taking her one step closer to her destination. The Jenolan

Caves and the Crucible of Doom. It seemed like an age since she had been at the palace, witnessing the disappearance of the Diamond, and she could never have predicted the chaos that had followed. She knew how important it was to protect Validor and earth from the Sable Witches and that if any one of them did not reach the Caves and the Crucible of Doom within the Devils Coach house, before the Sable Witches were able, it would be the end of Validor and Earth. This was not something she could live with. She was so close to being able to protect her family and the world from such a horrific event, all it needed was a last push. A final draw on all the energy and fight inside her tiny frame to get close to the crucible even though her muscles fought hard against her minds desire to find the caves. She pushed back with all her will and might, for her family, for her world and for their future. She squinted through the glare of the sun, trying to gain some perspective on how close to the caves she was. Her focused mind had been pinned steadfast to her feet willing them to keep placing one foot in front of the other. She had come so far, there was no way she would give up now. Soon her foot met a grey sun-bleached stone, then another and another. The stones did not look like the usual gravel scattered around the forest floor she had become accustomed to in her long race through the trees. The geology of the ground looked to be changing in front of her very eyes. The rocks becoming larger and more historic looking. She followed the path of rock as far as her eyes could see and as she did, she suddenly saw something, not more than fifty feet ahead of her, in all their charcoal rugged splendour. There they were, the magnificent Jenolan Caves. She could not believe how close she was. She was a whisker away from reaching them and had for half a second contemplated giving up. She was ecstatic that her weariness had not won the battle with her desire to do the right thing. Here she was, standing directly in front of the caves, ready to take on whatever difficulties she may meet in her path. Her fingers were red and sore from how tightly she had gripped the magic Ruby in her pocket She held it firmly in her palm to take from it some semblance of magic droplets of energy which would eventually bring her to the mouth of the caves. The arched sharp stone entrance beckoning her in. Inviting her to meet the hundreds of years of mystery surrounding the caves existence. She tiptoed into the cave, not wanting to bring attention to herself. After all, she did not know if she was the first to arrive, or if there were other living things inside this mystical place. She crept in, greeted by a wall of rainwater dripping down the stained walls of the shadowy cave. Her eyes met the Sapphire blue water of the river inside. This must have been the water she had heard when she had first taken her trip through the bushland. It was a breath-taking scene of shimmering green crystal-clear water, opening before her. Stalagmites and stalactites, standing on point from the floors and cave ceiling, what seemed like thousands of them, solid and erect with needlepoint sharpness, an army of icicle's all shapes and thickness, but all perfectly horizontal or vertical from their starting place. Ruby had never seen anything like this in all her life, and she was sure, she might never see anything similar again. The sheer beauty of this place, the wonders of Mother Nature which had created such a magical scene without the use of magic. Mother Nature, the true magician who had sculptured this fairy tale chamber. Ruby reached out to carefully touch one of the icicles. Not wanting to disturb it but intrigued to know how it felt. It was bitterly cold, and her fingers numbed in seconds. She let go and rubbed her hands together. Holding them close to her face, gently blowing into them, trying to generate some warmth. The temperature of her breath did not really help. The cave was sheltered from sunlight and the air chilled. She cautiously stepped to the brink of the sparkling river, her feet faltering on the uneven rock as she did. Crouching down, she dipped her hand in the still water, hoping the water was warmer than her breath. It swirled around her fingers as if caressing them and bringing them back to life. It was a tad warmer than her breath, and much more refreshing. The uplifting swirl of clean water around her hand sending reassuring messages through her soul that everything would be okay. Tiny momentary doubts emerging like mini bubbles in her head like, *can I do this alone, and is everyone okay?* Were washed away by the uplifting sway of the ripples swishing in her palm. The cave was serenity itself. The feint plop of water drops could be heard, rhythmically dripping like a faulty facet. Ruby glanced over each shoulder; she suddenly had the urge to climb into the river. Seduced by the sensation of the water against her hands, she wondered how it might feel to be totally immersed. She stood up and began to remove her top, then her pants, standing only in her starch white underwear, she dropped one pale slender leg into the lake, then the other. The water greeted her with a biting cool nip after an initial shiver, she quickly adjusted to the temperature as she became immersed into it to shoulder level. Her feet had not yet met the floor as the bed of the lake must have been deeper than her own body height. She tightly gripped the side of the riverbank with her hands to stay afloat.

Ruby cupped the cool water with her free hand and pushed it into her face, then repeated this until she felt she had washed the stress of recent days away. It was on the third scoop she felt the temperature of the water had become hot; it was almost burning her cheeks. She glanced across the water's surface. There was steam rising from it and the water had started to bubble, almost like a boiling pan. Ruby panicked and started to scramble out of the water and as she did, she felt her foot become lodged. She was unsure how it was trapped, but it was fixed firm and all her wriggling and writhing, could not free it.

'Help!' She yelled, unsure if there was anyone or anything around, but she had to try.

'Please help!'

The lake bubbled and frothed. Then suddenly a wave of hot water crashed over her head. Drenching her hair that had so far managed to remain dry up until that point. She coughed and spluttered as she began to draw in water through her gaping mouth and flaring nostrils. It was then she started to rise from the water, higher and higher until her head almost reached the cave roof. She pushed out her arms and tried to grab hold of something that might steady her. She spun her head desperately from side to side, trying to fathom what it was that had elevated her to such a height. He hands met something cold and slippery. She looked down and saw a large green something. Then pop, she jumped as a large red eyeball revealed itself and was looking directly at her. It was at that point she realised; she was on the shoulder of what looked like a large Dragon. Its nostrils filled with fire and teeth dripping with saliva. It began to speak.

'Why would I help you, you are in my lake, this is my home, and you were not invited?'

It had a female voice, feminine but foreboding. It began to flap its wings trying to unsteady Ruby from her position on its shoulders. Clearly very unhappy with the impromptu uninvited visit.

'Please stop, I mean you no harm, I did not know this was your river. Could you please stop moving and I will get out, I promise?'

The Dragon turned to look at her as best it could and with a sarcastic smile pretended to respond to Ruby's plea.

'Certainly, allow me to assist you', she said wryly. She lifted her short arm, revealing a long claw and flicked Ruby off her slimy green scaled shoulder.

Ruby launched into the air with space shuttle like speed, flying towards the cave entrance. She knew if she made impact with the cave wall, she would be sure to shatter into small pieces, but there was nothing she could do to slow down. Her tiny frame like a dandelion in a windstorm. Floating dangerously towards the cave roof and entrance. It was then she saw a dark shadow cross the entrance to the cave. Bringing the cave into total darkness and blocking a potential exit should Ruby have made it that far. But she didn't, because the blackout was followed by a sudden soft landing onto bouncy, rubbery type surface. In that moment, just as her brain was still trying to make sense of what had happened, she heard another sound. It was a deep wailing. A kind of cross between the howl of a wolf and an elephant's roar.

'Jump on!' A male voice insisted.

Ruby's sight adjusted to the point that she could see what she had landed on. A hand was outstretched in front of her, she glanced up to see the face that the hand belonged to. There she saw Daylin, his green eyes glinting in the light of the river, a gentle smile crossing his lips. It was then she realised she had landed on Nodrog's leg and Nodrog was in full flight into the cave entrance with the stealth of a Dragon warrior. Daylin offered his hand to pull Ruby onto Nodrog's back. Ruby did not need to be asked twice. She grasped his fingers as he began to wrench her with his strong forearm upwards.

'Climb girl, Climb!' an excited Sapphire urged.

Ruby found her way onto Nodrog's back. Soon realising the strange noise was emanating from Nodrog. She did not know he was even capable of such a sound. He was beginning to surprise her with each encounter. She noticed the other Dragon had responded to the sound by beginning to step slowly backwards away from the group and deeper into the cave. Sapphire was clapping Nodrog's back in delight and congratulating his successful rescue attempt. Ruby now sat directly in front of Daylin on Nodrog's back, his arms tightly around her waist, securing her safely into position. His two protective arms locking onto her delicate frame. Nodrog was still belting out the decibels and his peculiar moan. Now they were close up and personal with the other Dragon. An anxious expression passed over the other Dragon's face as they invaded its personal space. It started to wail in a similar tone to Nodrog's but more female in its sound. It was as though they were having a conversation. Nodrog was pitched a little higher than the other Dragon who was motionless flapping his wings to hold him in one place in the air. The noise was deafening, booming across the cave walls, reverberating as it did. Nodrog edged closer still. Then he tilted his head to one side as if observing something on the left of the other Dragon's head. The noise stopped, the other Dragon blinked with long eyelashes and wide eyes as if understanding what Nodrog had seen. It leant forward. Nodrog followed, he leaned in and began to lick around the other Dragon's face. Ruby could see what looked like black blood dripping from a cut which Nodrog had started to clean. The other Dragon had injured itself with all the commotion. It paused to let Nodrog continue, batting its eyelashes in appreciation and letting out a light sigh. Sapphire whispered.

'Well, I'll be damned. It's a female Dragon'

'She has pretty pink dots on her back too, see' Ruby exclaimed.

Daylin laughed.

'Well, well Nodrog, looks like you have found yourself a girlfriend. Now, come on Dotty, or whatever your name is, let us pass, we have important work to do. I promise I will bring your new friend back when this is over'

Nodrog gave a gentler groan now as if translating for Daylin. Dotty responded dutifully by dropping deeper into the water and shuffling to the side to allow them to pass through. Then suddenly the amnesty was interrupted by a whoosh of activity flying in from the cave entrance, cackles and shrieking voices, mains of raven black hair and cloaks, swooping in on glossy black broomsticks. It was the Sable Witches, going full throttle headed in the direction of both Dragons. One of them dragging on Sapphire's hair and becoming caught in it as they caught up. Sapphire was pulling desperately at her hair trying to release the bony cold hand of Yowla who had attached herself to her. Daylin was on his feet, perched on Nodrog's back thrashing out at each Witch who came within stone's throw of his heavy fists. He managed to grab the back of one of the broomsticks and fired. Whitney into the cave wall with a clatter. She slid into the water wearing a dazed expression. As she hit the water it turned into a complete sheet of Ice. Trapping both Dragons in it, Sapphire was still frantically trying to uncouple Yowla from her hair. Daylin wafted his arms as best he could trying to keep the others away from them. He turned to face Sapphire and Yowla and threw his arm across Yowla's broom stick to unbalance her from position, but instead he came crashing down onto the hard ice beneath. Leaving Sapphire and Ruby to fend for themselves. Sapphire followed Daylin, succumbing to the might of Yowla as she dragged her down to the ground. This left Ruby, hyperventilating and panic struck. A plague of bats had now joined them, circling around and joining in the battle. The Dragons were motionless, resigned to the fact that at this point they could not move. They rested their heads on one another as if comforting themselves. Daylin was holding his back, with his hand laid out on the hard ice surface. It had received quite a jolt as he had impacted the ice from a great height. The Sable Witches had created a sufficient distraction to allow them to continue their mission. King Organza ambled in at the end of the battle in an almost cowardly like manner, as if he had allowed his entourage to do the hard work for him. There was no way Organza would let a single hair be out of place in any form of confrontation! He quietly passed through from the back of the group.

'Enough of this, this is wasting time. Onward to the Crucible of Doom!' He yelled.

The other Sable Witches responded with a

'Hurrarah' and with turbo charged brooms disappeared into the distance.

Daylin shivered as his skin met the cold ice. His chin shook and his teeth clattered together. Sapphire tried to straighten the knots in her hair but was quivering alongside Daylin, she stammered.

'What now?'

Daylin blew warm air into his hands to defrost them.

'WWWWhat now, WWWhat now' he stammered

'Well, if these t t t two l l l love birds would snap out of it, they might come to the realisation that they could breathe fire!' He answered totally perplexed.

Ruby clapped her hand over her mouth in shock, she had also overlooked that special skill of theirs. She was still struggling to get used to a world of magic powers and Dragons. The Dragons looked unperturbed, still brushing their heads against one another, completely inseparable. Daylin cleared his throat in ready to speak, as though he was interrupting a romantic candle lit meal.

'Ahhhhmmmm, guys, if you do not mind, could you please.' He did not finish the sentence before Sapphire waded in.

'HEY, LOVE BIRDS, can you quit the canoodling and start some fires pronto. Melt this damn ice and get us the heck out of here!' She said far less tactfully than Daylin's earlier approach.

Daylin nodded, grabbing his shoulders with each hand as if holding himself.

'N N Nicely done Sapphire!'

Still the Dragons did not flinch, making warbling and gurgling noises, caught up in their own little world.

Ruby placed four fingers in her mouth letting out a shrill protracted whistle followed by

'FIRE, FIRE PLEEEEAAASE'

Nodrog jumped to attention and without any thought, automatically let out a stream of fire directly onto the ice, Dotty mirrored him, and they worked as a team blasting through it piece by piece. Slowly but surely, the ice began to turn to water once again, Daylin Sapphire and Ruby sheltered their eyes from the blue and orange flames which were too bright for the naked White Witch eye. Sapphire now immersed in the warm water, splashed over to Dotty. She clambered up her green slippery back and sat next to her neck. Dotty raised her eyes upwards, not quite sure what to make of this. This was not something she had experienced before. A Witch perched on her spine.

'Now, you should follow Nodrog, I will keep my eye on you so that you do not become distracted with each other' Sapphire said in a schoolteacher type voice.

Daylin was already back on Nodrog's back and ready to go.

'Follow those Witches!' He yelled. Nodrog vaulted into action, shadowed by a love-struck Dotty.

They trailed the path of the river, out to the other side of the cave where they found themselves directly in front of the Devils Coach House. The residence of the one and only Crucible of Doom. Swinging beneath its arches they dropped to the ground, scanning it for signs of Sable Witches. There they were, hunched in tiny balls on the floor, chanting loudly, they had just arrived in time. Their black cloaks splayed out around them in some kind of ritual. Red candles in black candelabras surrounding the crucible. King Organza was the only Sable Witch still standing. He was holding the Diamond high in the air, and it lit up like a prism. Shocks of colour tracing through it into the Crucible of Doom. There was still time, only when the ceremony had completed and when the Diamond meets the Crucible does the horror of Armageddon begin. This was the one thing Ruby had remembered from her conversation with Emperor Zilante. They looked on, remaining quiet so as not to alert the others to their presence.

'What now?' Whispered Sapphire into Daylin's ear

'Honestly, I have no idea' Daylin murmured, eyes transfixed on the ceremony below them

Fortunately, Ruby had already begun a plan in her head

'First, we must take the Diamond, then we must trap them so that we can return it to the Precipice of Peace in Lucas Cave'

Daylin scratched his head

'The P ppp of what, what on earth is that?'

'It is the place the Diamond must remain to keep calm and Peace on earth and in Validor until a new Queen is found'. She replied in a calm and hushed voice.

Nodrog responded by blowing himself up to appear twice his natural size, flapping his wings in a macho man

Dragon type way, whilst winking at Dotty. He then soared into the sky, and immediately headed back down, directly towards Organza as fast as his wings would carry him. He moved at the pace of a fighter plane, locked firmly onto his target, the Diamond of Lucas Cave. He swooped in, grabbed the Diamond between his teeth, and then launched back upwards out of reach of the others. Dotty had her own ideas, she had been busily collecting the Sable Witches brooms in her mouth one by one, then cascading them deep into the forest. They were both a cute and formidable team, the Dragon couple. This was the moment for Ruby to step in, she clung to her Ruby and began to put mental images of each of the Sable Witches through her mind. Then one by one, she mentally threw each one into the walls of her Ruby.

Daylin could not believe what he was seeing. Each of the Sable Witches began hurtling through the air towards Ruby, but as each one reached her, they shrunk to the size of a penny, then disintegrated. It all happened so quickly, Daylin was sure it was an illusion. Sapphire blurted out first.

'Whoooah, what is happening?'

'I have no idea?' Replied a very confused looking Daylin.

'I don't like to ask' he continued, barely moving his mouth as he spoke.

Daylin, stood frozen to the spot. Too afraid to move. There was far too much magic floating around for his liking, and he did not want to be a victim of it. Once the last of the Sable Witches had disappeared, Ruby slumped to the floor.

'Are you okay?' Sapphire asked Ruby, looking extremely concerned.

'Yes, I am now, thank you' she replied panting with each word.

'I don't get it' Daylin said. 'What happened to the Sable Witches?' He searched the ground below him. There was no trace of them.

'They are in here' Ruby said, shaking the Ruby in mid-air. Dotty had settled down next to Nodrog now and the group were seated close together catching their breath. Sapphire snatched the Ruby from her and stared into it, shaking her head she passed it to Daylin. They both could not believe their eyes, sure enough, all the Sable Witches were trapped in the Ruby and standing next to them were the three sisters. All trying to thump their way out. It looked like some kind of bad miniature silent movie.

'Well done girl, you are really getting the hang of this magic business' Sapphire said, congratulating Ruby on a job well done.

'Thank you, but we are not quite finished. We need to get the Diamond back to the Precipice of Peace'

Daylin nodded, not wanting to argue.

'Whatever you say Ruby. Whatever you say.' He gently planted a kiss on her unsuspecting cheek bringing her round from her trancelike state. She touched her cheek as if reflecting on what had just happened. Then looked to the floor before her face began to flush pink.

CHAPTER 15

REUNITED

Moonstone and Morganite yawned and stretched into life after a long siesta, still a little confused about where they were. How did anyone become trapped in a Werewolves slimy dark intestine they thought? It seemed like such nonsense. Although it was a desolate place to be, their bed of pink skin was warm spongy and soft which was small consolation.

'Any new ideas about how we could get out of here?' Moonstone asked apathetically.

'Not really, all I can think is that he will be hungry soon. If we time it right, when he opens his mouth to eat, we could jump back out'

Moonstone, scoffed at the notion.

'You want us to climb back up, then sit amongst his razor-sharp teeth and wait until he decides to open his mouth. That is what you are suggesting right?'

Morganite scowled before replying.

'Pretty much, unless you have a better idea?' Moonstone stood up, dusting down her crumpled pants.

'Nope, sounds crazy to me, but if I must stay in here a minute longer, I think I will burst. So, I am in. Let's do it'

Morganite tried to get up and lost his footing in the hurry.

'Oh okay, didn't think you would be up for it. You surprised me somewhat. Okay, well, let's go?'

He crouched on one knee and patted it, beckoning to Moonstone that she should step on, and he would then push her up the tunnel of intestine. Moonstone, did as she was encouraged, thrusting herself upwards, using Morganite's knee as a springboard. Morganite made a less athletic attempt to follow, sliding up the intestine as best he could with very little to grip onto. Snaking their way upwards. Every now and then stopping to look at each other for inspiration. Puffing and panting their way up, with dogged determination. Both knowing this was their last and only hope.

They could see the Werewolf's mostly shiny white teeth ahead of them, some covered with yellow stains and dripping spit. It was not the most welcoming place they had found themselves in. Once again, they looked at each other, grimacing in unison. Morganite gave a shrug of his shoulders as if to say, we have come this far. They both managed to find a spot behind a rotten black back molar, each on the opposite side of the wolf's mouth. They gave a thumbs up as they wriggled into a hidden spot. An hour passed, then another. Moonstone was furiously signing to Morganite that she thought they should give up and go back down. She gestured with a chop across her neck, then pointed downwards. Morganite shook his head rigorously in response. He was adamant that his plan would work. It just needed patience. Moonstone slumped back against her charcoal black tooth seat in protest and as she did, her unballerina like coordination sent her slipping into the wolf's giant punch bag tonsil. On hitting it, the Werewolf began to cough, then coughed again until he sucked in a deep breath and gave a final hard cough, the wind from his throat like a gale force. It immediately flung Morganite and Moonstone out into the open air. They were travelling so fast; they could barely see what they were passing. It was like trying to make sense of your surroundings whilst travelling on a high-speed train reaching hundreds of miles per hour, which eventually lost momentum. Morganite opened one eye. Both of his eyes had been firmly closed for the entire flight. This was one fairground ride he did not need to see. He looked down as he felt himself start to drop; he could see dark shapes below him. As he grew closer, he knew for sure, it was the Jenolan Caves. He shook his head in disbelief. Almost as if he thought he was seeing things, but no, the caves were there, directly beneath his feet.

They crashed to the floor, first Morganite then Moonstone letting out a groan as they did. Morganite felt his back crack against the floor. Moonstone crushed her elbow as she came to her own unladylike landing.

'Owwww' they both yelped in chorus.

They carefully sat up, checking they were still able to. Moonstone touched her arms and legs to make sure everything was still in one piece.

'All present and correct sir' she joked to a stunned Morganite. Morganite nodded. He lacked the energy or lung capacity to speak at this point.

He carefully lifted a sluggish eyelid. There were branches gently swaying above his head, making light whispering swishing sound as the leaves on each branch met. Shifting his gaze to the left a little he saw a grinning Moonstone leaning over him, hands on hips.

'So, next stop Jenolan caves then?' She said with the enthusiasm of a six-year-old going to the park to play.

Morganite carefully sat upright on the floor. Still a little tender from their crash landing. He began drinking in the scenery around him.

'I guess so, if we …?'

'Shhh' Moonstone replied rather rudely. She pushed her fingers against her temple in contemplation, eyes firmly shut. Morganite recognized the signs and remained quiet. Moonstone must be receiving a psychic message in her mind. A few moments passed and Moonstone slowly opened her eyes, as if waking from a deep sleep.

'We must go deeper into the forest before we go to the caves. Emerald has asked us to save a family that is being held captive by the Sable Witches'

Morganite shook his head in disbelief

'You cannot be serious; we are literally steps away from the caves?'

'Deadly serious, and we are also only steps away from the place where the family is being held prisoner, albeit in the opposite direction.

Morganite sighed reluctantly, standing up and dusting off his hands.

'Very well, show me the way'

Moonstone nodded her head with a quick jolt and set off walking. Taking firm and purposeful steps towards her new mission. Moonstone pointed at a large set of boulders that looked to have been piled on top of one another in a contrived and unnatural way. She pressed one finger on her mouth as if to say 'quiet' Then started to lift the top boulder from the pile, then the next, then the next. Morganite began to imitate her, and the pile gradually became lower and lower before their eyes. When they removed the last grey dusty boulder, they saw what looked like the entrance to something below ground level.

'What's in there?' Whispered Morganite

'A mother and two children, the Unmerciful Mummies family. The Sable Witches got word that the Mummy had been befriended by Emerald. They knew it was a matter of time until we came looking for them. They hid them in this tomb stone hoping that they were never found'

Morganite was lost for words. Totally dumbstruck at such a callous act even by the Sable Witches standards. He leant down peering into the cavity in the floor. At first, he could see nothing but darkness. He rubbed his palms together and began to breathe into them, muttering strange words as he did. Moments later a bolt of fire light jumped from his hand and hovered only millimeters from his palm. He steered his hand into the hole in the ground, as he did the fire lit the entrance and the cavity beneath. There below him he could see three pairs of innocent blue eyes and soot covered black faces. It was a woman and two children, dressed in rags and looking emaciated. Morganite knew there was no time to lose. He reached for his Morganite stone and began to chant again, this time much louder. The children leaned into their mother's arm pit for safety whilst she tried to give the fiercest glare to the new visitors. It was the best deterrent she could muster as she was so weak, she could not move a limb and she was unsure if their new visitors were dangerous. Morganite blew into his palm once more and from his hands floated, banana's, apples, oranges, peaches, melons all in a uniformed lined they moved through the air, floating to the floor of the cave, coming to a rest next to the hand of the mother. The mother looked on her eyes wide with disbelief, puzzled at what had just happened. Who were these people, was this fruit real, was she dreaming? Her mind had become increasingly suspicious since her ordeal with the Sable Witches, she no longer knew who she could trust. Whilst she was trying to comprehend what was happening, her hungry children had grabbed the fruit and began cramming it into their parched mouths. The juice of the fruit running down each of their chins and dripping to the cave floor.

'It's okay' Moonstone smiled.

'We are here to help. Your husband sent us. He wants you to know he is okay and with friends'

The mother nodded, starting to tear into an orange. She had lost the battle in her mind which said she should not eat, and her hunger had won.

More fruit started to fill the cave entrance, enough fruit to last for days, maybe weeks. The children gave grateful smiles whilst their mother stroked their hair maternally, in a way that let them know everything was going to be okay.

'I know this is not a nice place to be right now, but you must stay here for a little longer. You are safer here. The Sable Witches are at large, and I and my White Witch friend need to deal with this, do you understand?' Morganite said in a serious manner.

The mother nodded once more; her mouth filled with succulent fruit.

'Don't worry, we will cast a spell on the entrance so that is looks to have disappeared. When it eventually re-opens, that will mean you are safe to go home. In other words, we have defeated the Sable Witches. It won't be long'

Moonstone gave a warm smile and reached in to touch the children's hands.

'Do not be afraid, all is going to be okay. You will all be together as a family soon. We promise?'

With that they both pressed their heads together, forehead to forehead. Then brought the Morganite and Moonstone together. Morganite's left hand meeting Moonstones right hand. Then in a magical precious jewel flash, the entrance to the cavity disappeared, at least to the Sable Witch eye anyway. Morganite and Moonstones hand clashed together in a celebratory slap in a job well done.

'Okay, now let us get to the caves' Morganite said sternly, secretly glad that he had been able to help, but keen to get back to their mission. They spun around on their heels and began to run back towards the beautiful grey caves they had seen when they had been in flight minutes earlier. The caves started to look taller as they became closer to them. *Such a stunning work of art made by nature*, Morganite thought, not a drop of magic involved in their creation, yet there they were a craggy sculpted masterpiece of grey stone rising tall above the ground. Breathless they arrived at the cave wall. Now close enough to touch. Morganite set about trying to find an entrance, peering through each crack that produced a ray of sunlight through it. This ritual went on for several minutes. Moonstone scratched her tatty head of hair.

'Well, we can keep doing this until darkness reaches us, or we can do the reverse of the magic we did before to seal the family in?'

'Already thought of that, it would create a disturbance and bring attention to us being there. We may run straight into the Sable Witches' he muttered, desperately searching his intellect for a better idea. As he did, he touched each crevice of the wall as if feeling for a way in. He had almost gone down one side of the cave and disappeared from Moonstone's line of vision when he yelled

'I have found a way in, we may have to climb a little and squeeze through a gap, but I think it could work!'

Moonstone followed his voice until she way directly beneath him. He had already begun to expertly scale the cave wall. She started to trace his footsteps, one ledge after the other in a calm but methodical manner. Eventually they were directly in front of a body sized opening, although it was an exceedingly small body shaped opening indeed. Morganite began to edge in, first with his shoulder, gently navigating the rest of his body through the tiny gap. His skin scrapping against the sharp edges of the rock as he did. Moonstone was immediately behind him, cramming herself in behind him like they were fighting their way onto the London tube train at rush hour. Morganites face flushed red, mostly from exertion but also, he was a tad annoyed that Moonstone had not found the patience to wait until he had made it through himself before making the climb. After crushing his whole being into a tiny crevice Morganite found himself falling through the air on the inside of the cave, dropping at a rate of knots until he crashed to the floor with a bone shattering thud. Immediately followed by an untidy bundle of Moonstone. Both still wearing the slimy content of the werewolf's unhygienic mouth. Splashes of saliva hitting the floor around them like the spray from a dog who had begun shaking himself from a swim in a dirty lake. Moonstone's stomach turned as her body writhed up and then down on the floor. She knew she had landed, but the waves up and down of her torso had started to make her feel nauseous.

'Why am I moving?' She questioned out loud, her arms and legs flaying uncontrollably in the air.

'Because' gasped Morganite

'You landed on top of me, and it really hurt!' He said, rather annoyed that not only has she been cushioned by him when landing, but she also had not really been appreciative of his accidental gesture.

'I am so sorry Morganite, it really wasn't something in my control'

Morganite gave one final jolt of his body, this time throwing Moonstone onto the grass.

'Ooof, thank you' Moonstone blurted out, with a hint of sarcasm.

'My pleasure' smiled Morganite, relieved that her weight had been lifted from him.

'Now we are even!' He smiled.

'Impressive entrance guys, but where on earth did you come from?'

A big booming friendly female voice asked. Morganite swung round in the direction of the voice to find a round faced Sapphire leaning over them. She began to laugh that all familiar heartwarming laugh.

'Sapphire, it's you, my, you are a sight for sore eyes' said Moonstone

'Are we glad to see you!' Morganite joined in.

Sapphire threw her chunky chocolate brown arms around both of their necks almost bashing their heads together as she did. They both smiled at the scene, quite accustomed to these warm loving gestures from Sapphire.

'Tell me Sapphire, what did we miss?' Morganite inquired earnestly.

Ruby appeared beside Sapphire her eyes gleaming with the appearance of their long-lost friends.

'Well, you missed this for a start' she said with a proud glint in her eye, she raised the Ruby up above their heads so that it caught a stream of light streaming through the gap in the cave wall. There they saw a team of angry Sable Witches and the three now very cross sisters.

'Wow, you really are getting the hang of this magic thing. Well done Ruby!' Moonstone gushed. Alex strolled up alongside them, beaming from ear to ear.

'Guys, so glad you are safe. I know we have so much to catch up on, but we do not have much time I am afraid. We really need to get the Diamond to the Precipice of Peace'

Morganite raised his arms high in the air as if making a plea to the heavens.

'Sure Alex, but if I don't wash this goo off soon, I think it will interfere with any magic I might try to create' he shook his clothes as if demonstrating how scaly and crusty they had become.

Alex looked them both up and down and his jaw set.

'Fine, we really do not have the time, but' he waved his shovel like hand towards the lake urging them to quickly get in. He slumped back onto a ledge next to the lake and the others followed suit. Each one shaking the ledge each time their weight landed on it. Moonstone dove in first with the agility of an Olympic swimmer, followed by a belly flopping Morganite. They were surprised at how warm and refreshing the water was. They had no inkling that only hours earlier, it had been a bath of ice, then fire.

♟♟♟

The mermaid raced over to where Alex and Pearl were standing. Her once calm demeanor slightly ruffled with the events of the evening. Still wearing the beautiful alluring smile she had shown when she first greeted each one of them. The slight frown in the middle of her forehead revealing the anxiety behind the smile.

'You must go, Astro is using his magic to place clam palace in permanent lock down. I am afraid, if he is successful, you will not survive it. Humans and White Witches are not physically designed to stay here for too long' she pleaded.

Alex and Pearl went into panic mode, desperately searching the walls around them for a way out. Swinging one way and then the next, Pearls raven black hair flying through the air at the same rapid pace at each turn of her head. The smiling mermaid came between them and revealed a clam shell which she placed over both of their mouths to demonstrate how to use them, then removed them.

'Take the shells, they will help you breath on your journey through the water'

She turned to Pearl opening her mouth wide. Pearl stared into her petite youthful mouth to see pure white tonsils shaped as Pearls. The same tonsils that she had seen so many times in her own mouth whilst looking in the mirror. It was at that very moment she realized the origin of her own Pearl, and that the mermaids and Clam Palace must be part of her family and heritage. She had so many questions but no time to ask or find the answers. The smiling mermaid gently closed her mouth before saying.

'Pearl open your mouth in the same way I do so that our tonsils are aligned please'

Pearl scrunched her eyes up, puzzled at the request, but she had come to trust her beautiful new friend. She turned to face her and opened her mouth, as instructed and as soon as their tonsils lined up, Pearl was greeted by directions and images of the sea flying through her head. There were maps upon maps layered across the waves in the sea. Each wave representing a mini motorway. Pearl's mind was racing, her chest bursting with elation at what she was learning in those brief illuminating nano seconds. It was the world's best kept secret which brought a totally new perspective to how Pearl saw the sea. She was so thrilled that she had been thought special enough to learn this privileged intelligence and, as we have learned, Pearl is exceedingly difficult to impress. Each wave of the sea was a motorway, a clear direction to another place. All you needed to know was how to read it, only mermaids, sea animals, and now Pearl had the magical power to do this. The smiling mermaid clamped her mouth shut, pushed her forehead against Pearls, taking her face into her delicate mermaid hands.

'Now go!'

Pearl, nodded, she understood that they must go, and that they must go now.

'Alex, place the clam shell over your mouth. I know the way to Lucas Cave by water, follow me' she said. She led him to the scrubbed clean clam wall where a crack was clearly visible. They both slid through it effortlessly, one after the other into the deep azure blue depths of the sea and into the hands of the sea gods (if there is such a thing).

🎎🎎🎎

'Watch this!' Moonstone shouted playfully. Throwing herself under the deep green water once more, this time in a handstand. Morganite gave a disapproving tut as he rubbed under his clothed arms trying to get clean through his clothes. Then, she disappeared completely into the depths of the lagoon. Little bubbles appearing at the top where she once stood. The others quickly stood up, scanning the surface of the water with their eyes, faces etched with intense concern. A solemn thirty seconds passed before up she popped, the others shook their heads at how alarmed they had been and dropped back in their seats.

'Get off my ankle! It's not funny anymore!' Moonstone puffed, trying to keep her head above water.

'It so is!' Said a male voice half laughing. The others gasped in disbelief as a very blond, handsome, water clad Alex appeared next to Moonstone in the lake, immediately followed by the slender and sleek Pearl. Pearl was the first to start dragging herself out of the water, her dark hair gripping the nape of her neck as she did. She was clearly bemused at the whole experience. They had navigated themselves through the sea maps with only their shell to breath, as fast as their bodies and magic would carry them.

'Okay, parties over. Take me to the unstable Sables, let me sort this out once and for all' she commanded wringing her hair out with both hands freeing it of a mass of water onto the cave floor.

Ruby stepped forward, feeling this was another moment to shine and prove she really was a White Witch in every sense. She held the Ruby in Pearls line of vision.

'All done Pearl, our work is almost complete!'

Pearl snatched the Ruby from Pearls hand examining it carefully. Still dripping wet with a pool of water forming in a puddle.

'It's impossible to hold them there forever' she replied icily, trying firmly to burst the bubble of positivity in the group.

'Pearls right actually, although I think she might have said it in a kinder way. We need to get the Diamond to the Precipice of Peace as soon as we can. That at least secures the future of the world and Validor' chimed in Daylin. He gave Ruby's shoulder a gentle squeeze to let her know he still thought she had done a great job.

Alex bent down wringing out his soggy socks followed by a surprised and curious look up.

'You mean we have the Diamond too?'

They all said 'yes' in unison, followed by a burst of laughter at how uncanny that was. Pearl glanced around the room, she was secretly pleased they were all safe and in one piece. She suspected they all had a tale of woe to share, but now was not the right moment. It was then she realized there was a familiar face missing from their merry group.

'Wait, where is Opal?' She asked

Ruby looked at the floor reminded of the horror of what had happened to Opal at her mothers' home. Daylin, gave her shoulder a squeeze once more, he had seen how she had tensed at the mention of Opals name and sensed her guilt.

'Opal is safe, she is in Scotland. We will make sure she is okay once more, when we have returned the Diamond' said Daylin with a voice of authority which was unusual for him.

'No need for a rescue party, I am here already gdday. I have missed you all heaps!' Said a strong Australian accent echoing across the walls of the cave. There in the cave doorway stood Opal. Ruby sat back down on the ledge clutching her chest in a mixture of surprise and relief at Opals sudden reappearance.

'Did something happen to the Three Sisters, I mean, one minute I was frozen in ice, the next I was dancing around the garden in the sun?' Queried Opal.

'Look, girls, girls, as much as I am as excited about this reunion as the next person. Interjected Pearl, we really do not have time to chat. We need to get the Diamond to the precipice!'

'For once I agree with you. I am in, and I can show you the way!' Said Opal, full of unspent renewed energy since her melt down. She marched forward along the aisle beside the shimmering green lake, travelling deeper and deeper into the body of the cave. They began to climb what looked like a natural stone staircase and the scenery became more and more spectacular with every step. Marching in a uniformed line, they were all completely fixed on fulfilling Queen Diamond's wishes before she was banished to White Swan Lake. This is the least they could do for the Queen that had cared for each one of them throughout their life. This was their time to pay her back. They were blown away with their whole surroundings. Never had they seen such a magical place, and for a team of White Witches who had been raised on phenomenal displays of magic, this was quite astonishing.

CHAPTER 16

THE PRECIPICE OF PEACE

They knew it when the saw it. It could not be mistaken. There it was, a perfect line of stone, with a look of frozen fur, a rippling stone that looked like it was dripping from the ceiling but in a solid state. If you followed the stone down it was as though someone had taken a bite out of its once perfectly formed single line of stone. It had the nobbles and drips of a melted candle hanging down from the cave wall, in a beige like sand. The whole stone community surrounding it was moonlike with an air of eeriness. The precipice itself was between the long and the short part of the stone structure. The joining of a stalagmite and stalactite. It was such a delicate formation, there was every chance the Witches may dislodge some or part of it if they worked in haste. It was so close they could reach out and touch it. Daylin ripped off the diamond which had been tied to a black lace around his neck for safe keeping. The lace snapped evenly and fell to the floor. The Diamond now tightly in Daylin's grasp.

'I cannot do this; my hand is too heavy and the gap too difficult to navigate. It needs a smaller hand' he said like a doctor contemplating a surgical procedure.

'I can do it!' Moonstone leapt in. Her hand was delicate and tiny sure enough.

'No, you are far too clumsy. I will do it,' said Pearl.

'Actually, it is Daylin that must do it. Really sorry Pearl, I am not sure why, but that is what Emperor Zilante told me this when he visited me in my dream' Ruby said sheepishly. Daylin gave a half smile, impressed at the strength Ruby was starting to show in her new role as a White Witch. He opened his hand and holding the Diamond firmly in it, he gave it a quick squeeze and nodded as if to say *its time*. He reached forward his wrist slightly shaking with the weight of the Diamond in his grip. Ruby grabbed his other hand which was lying still against his leg to steady him. He continued to edge his hand forward until the Diamond was directly between the stalagmite and stalactite. As it reached the correct location it began to glow and float in midair, shocks of white and blue light passing through it. Almost blinding the Witches as they looked on in amazement. Daylin retracted his hand, shielding his eyes from the starkness of the ray of magical light. The others turned away for fear the light might damage their eyes. The ground started to shake beneath their feet, and the flashes of light began to buzz like a broken power line. The Witches tried to keep their balance as the ground shifted beneath their feet. The cave walls began to shake and creak a little. Then, nothing. The cave fell into silence and the Diamond sat like it had found its true home floating between the high and low of the stalagmite and stalactite. Ruby let out the breath she felt she had been holding for an eternity. The others clapped and cheered, wrapping their arms around each other. It was finally over, the world and Validor was safe once more.

'Well, all is well in the world, now it's time to head back home!' Morganite smiled.

'But before we do, I have something I really need to say' Daylin said quietly. The Witches stopped their chatter. They knew Daylin to be a man of few words so his message must be important. He still had hold of Ruby's hand and had deliberately not released it.

'Ruby, I am so very much in love with you, and I need to know, if you would do me the honor of becoming my wife. I cannot go on living my life, without you in it!'

The others gasped and giggled in excitement.

He paused for a moment, digging into his trouser pocket. Once he had found what he sought, he lifted his hand out and opened it in front of Ruby. There he revealed his father's shiny gold pocket watch. He gently unclipped the clasp revealing his mother's beautiful diamond engagement ring. He carefully took it from its place of safety, and gently slid it onto Ruby's tiny finger, and, as if my magic, it fit perfectly.

'Daylin, I would love to be your wife, but how? You are not of White Witch blood and we both know the rules?'

'No, he does not have White Witch blood, his blood line is far superior. Daylin's mother Wyveen was a child of the Emperor and Empress of the Dragons. That means, he is royalty Ruby, and you can be married!' Sapphire blurted out, not wanting to confess to having eaves dropped on the conversation between Daylin and his father Duke. Morganite began to slowly clap joining in the celebration.

'Well, I will be damned, Empress Ruby indeed?' He shook his head, not quite believing what he had learned.

Ruby and Daylin were locked in a kiss, oblivious to the presence of the other Witches around them. The claps and whistles grew louder as they stayed entwined in each other's arms. The glow of the Diamond lighting the area around them up like they were on stage beneath a spotlight. Suddenly, there was the sound of heavy footsteps on the floor beneath them, heavy enough to rock the cave walls once more. It was dotty the Dragon, Daylin felt a pang of remorse, he had left the love birds outside as they were too caught up in each other to be of any help. Dotty wore a perplexed expression and sweat dripped down her face from her rapid entrance into the cave. Once she reached the Witches, she stopped gasping for breath.

'What is it Dotty, is everything okay?' Daylin asked suddenly releasing from his embrace with Ruby. Dotty struggled to show them what had happened, but clearly distressed with the events which had unfolded whilst the Witches had been busy in the cave.

'Anyone speak Dragon?' Pearl asked sarcastically. Moonstone pushed her way through, giving Pearl an icy stare.

'I will handle this; I just need to get into her head'

She placed one finger on each temple with each hand and tried to tune into Dotty's mind. The others remained silent allowing her to focus on the psychic messaging.

Moonstone flashed open her eyes before bursting into floods of tears.

'It's, Its Nodrog, I think he is dead' she blubbered.

CHAPTER 17

DRAGONS IN LOVE

"Dead, Dead but how?" Daylin stammered. Ruby took his hand rubbing his fingers to comfort him fighting back her own tears at the same time.

'A pack of hungry evil wolves fought him to the ground, then dragged him away,' cried Moonstone.

Daylin did not need any further information. He pounced into action, Nodrog was dear friend of his, a member of his family even. He would do everything within his power to save him.

'Dotty, take me to the place where you last saw him' Daylin insisted. Dotty dropped her head low revealing her ladder like neck. Daylin began to scale her sturdy neck being careful not to scrape her with his hands are shoes, avoiding the soft pink spots which were her namesake. She hurled herself into a run, knowing that every second might make the difference to Nodrog's survival. The others stood in silent devastation, feeling a little hopeless. They knew a partnership of Dotty and Daylin was a formidable one, but all the same, Daylin had no magical abilities, could he really save Nodrog. Morganite looked across the sea of shocked faces. He decided it would be best if he took control, and quickly.

'I know what you are thinking, but Daylin has made it this far and the love for Nodrog between the two of them will be enough to keep him safe'

Ruby had her hand over her open mouth, still trying to comprehend what just happened. It was the happiest and saddest moment of her life all ground into one. Pearl wrapped her arm around Ruby's shoulders, for a brief moment revealing a softer side to her hard exterior.

Dotty ran across the beige stone path on all fours. Daylin clinging on tightly and leaning his torso against her neck they cleared the entrance to the cave with a duck of his head. It was a good thing he saw it coming because its jagged edging might have taken his head clean off. They raced across the dirt track and into a tree lined area. Dotty skillfully navigating her way around each one, she showed such grace for an animal of her size. Her feet skidding in the dust as she turned from left to right. Daylin leaning in with each turn like a motorbike rider in a speedway race. Puffs of smoke billowing out of her nostrils, a reflection of the energy she was spending in this elegant canter. Eventually, she rose into the sky elevated over the treetops, It was like the forest had been her runway and she was a large aircraft. Daylin scoured the floor beneath, trying to find even the slightest trace of Nodrog, in any shape or form. A footprint, a body print, anything really, if it was a sign that Nodrog been present for any length of time. He even investigated the area for wolf tracks, or as far as he could see at the distance he was at. They flew for miles, and hours. Dotty began to show signs of fatigue, her body no longer flying at one height. She raised, then dropped, raised, then dropped. Giving Daylin the feeling of being on a roller coaster. He saw this as a time to stop, and just as he made the mental decision to quit, he saw a pack of wolves around half a mile ahead of him.

'Dotty, look, look ahead, there is a pack of wolves. Please drop to the ground'

Dotty gave a slow lethargic nod, she looked up into his eyes as if to say, if you are sure. She was trusting Daylin to be able to keep them both safe. She began to drop down, gradually losing height and closing in on the group of wolves and as they grew closer, she could hear their barks. They had seen Dotty coming and their jaws and mouths dripped with blood, gaping into the sky as if waiting to receive their next victim. Sure enough, their appearance had created a gap in their tightly made circle of fur, and between the gaps, they could see a motionless Nodrog, he was bleeding heavily from around his neck. The wolves turned back to look at Nodrog, it was clear he was going to be their next meal and in not too much time. Dotty landed softly on the ground, her hind legs first, followed by her front. Her back legs dragging them to a halt, creating a cloud of dust. Two wolves had sauntered over, backs arched and snarling, giving them both an evil and hostile greeting on landing. Dotty struck the first blow, both wings simultaneously hurling the wolves through the air and for miles into the distance. Daylin, gave her a pat on the head filled with gratitude, then slid down. He was impressed that Dotty had found the energy to bat them off but knew that the wolves had a hundred more wolves remaining and he had no clue how they would be able to get through them. His feet met the ground, and he began to run towards them, with no regard for his own safety. Dotty was steps behind him, tired from the long flight, but still battling through it. He reached the wolves, still barking and sneering, blood dripping from their teeth, even their faced splattered with the remnants of their earlier kills, or at least that is what Daylin hoped, he could not face the thought that this might be Nodrog's blood. They snapped at his legs as he passed them, Daylin danced through them unscathed, like a footballer dodging threw lessor skilled opponents. As he reached Nodrog's tail, he noticed that two wolves were about to take a bite from Nodrog's motionless body.

'NOOOOOOOO !!!' screamed Daylin and as he did, a cloud of smoke puffed from his mouth. He tried it again, taking himself by surprise at where this smoke was coming from

'NOOOOOOOOO, STOP RIGHT NOW!' He yelled again. Suddenly his scream became a roar. A roar like one he had only every heard come from Nodrog in the past, the roar was uncontrollable, coming from somewhere deep within his chest. Suddenly, the roar and the smoke was replaced by a wall of fire, coming directly out of his mouth. He didn't turn his head from the target, but his eyes met Dotty's filled with total confusion. It was not something he was feeling comfortable with, but it was everything he needed right now. He looked down at his hands and he saw that his hands were turning a golden colour and his fingers had become claws. He looked at his feet, now giant and flipper like, his legs golden and covered in scales. He had grown at least twenty feet and towered above the wolf pack. Daylin was no longer the Daylin everyone knew and loved, Daylin was now Daylin, the Dragon Emperor. He began to flick the tiny miniature wolves away from his wounded friend. They were no longer a match for a magical creature of Daylin's strength. Dotty was seated next to Nodrog and licking his wound clean, trying to stop the flow of blood which she did to a certain extent. The wolves yelped under the force of the stream of fire and began to run away, far amongst the trees for shelter. Once each one had disappeared, Daylin lay flat on the floor next to Nodrog. He was still in Dragon form and nuzzled his head against Nodrog, gently pushing his head, trying to get some kind of response. There was nothing. He dropped his head onto Nodrog's for a moment, totally traumatized at Nodrog's listlessness. He moved to the front of Nodrog and gently shuffled underneath him. Once Nodrog was lying across Daylin he stood on all fours and began to run with him before breaking into a stealth like flight through the air. Dotty followed, using the last bit of strength she could muster. They floated like a feather on the breeze for miles. There was some kind of magical force carrying them quickly back to the cave. Daylin was unsure if this was Dragons powers or if the White Witches were behind it somehow. Either way, he was so very grateful. All he could think of was returning his dear friend to the cave. He was still unsure if Nodrog was dead or alive, it was difficult to tell. The cave was upon them, so they started to descend to the ground. They came to a landing close to the cave entrance. Daylin hitting the dry soil first. It was quite a steady landing considering this was not something he had ever done before. The long flight had given him time to think about how he had changed, and where his ability to be a Dragon had come from. The only logical explanation was that it was part of his ancestry and that when his own or a loved one's life felt threatened, he would change into Dragon form. Perhaps it was emotionally driven, or maybe because he had finally found the woman he would marry, this meant his powers had now become more visible. His only question was how and if he would ever return to human form. Then, as if something had read his mind, his question was answered. As his feet met the ground, he saw his hands and feet start to return to human form. He slowly rolled Nodrog to the ground next to him, feared he may crush him if he returned to his former self. He was totally transformed back to Daylin the man and just in time. As he did, Ruby appeared in the cave entrance, she had felt the tremor of their landing through the walls of the cave and headed in the direction of the noise. The others only a few steps behind her.

'Oh no, is he okay?' She asked staring at the seemingly lifeless on the floor.

'We don't know' choked Daylin, wringing his hands which felt a little stiff from the long flight. He turned away from the group, not wanting them to see the tears in his eyes. He looked to the floor.

'Is, Is there anything, any of you can do for him?'

Pearl stepped forward first, pressing her hand to Nodrog's neck. She sat there for around ten seconds, before rising and stepping slowly backwards.

'I am afraid he is dead' she said in a quiet somber voice.

'NOOOOOO!' Moonstone wailed, flopping down next to his head.

Ruby buried her head in Daylin's shoulder and began to sob uncontrollably. Morganite placed a hand on his back, stroking it gently.

'Goodbye my dear friend, we will never forget you'

Opal kicked the floor with her boots.

'This really sucks' she said in a voice broken with grief.

Dotty rested her head across his, big droplets of tears falling from her big eyes which rolled down her own cheek, then Nodrog's.

'Okay, well there is nothing more we can do here. We need to leave him at peace in the cave. He can stay with the Diamond, where he belongs. We can call him Nodrog keeper of the Diamond, we will tell his story for years to come. He will be a legend. We will make sure of it!' Morganite said as positively as he could'

Dotty used all her weight to push Nodrog to shelter in the cave entrance.

Morganite took the lead once more.

'Now, let us sit out here and reflect a little on our friend and send out our love and thoughts to him. All of us except you Moonstone. I think you need a little more time to say goodbye'

Moonstone was still crouched close to Nodrog. She knew what Morganite wanted, she had the power to resurrect life after death, but her powers could not be displayed in front of Daylin. Not yet anyway. She was not really crying; she just created the dramatic display so she could get close to Nodrog and start to work her special magic. The others walked in procession into the cave. Morganite guided them to the exit with his arms wide like a police officer managing a large crowd. He looked back over his shoulder to Moonstone, gave a quick nod and a wink. Moonstone returned the nod, then buried her head back in her hands to continue the show.

They reached the blue lake in all its sparkling splendor, and even this could not raise a smile from the others. They could not quite believe what had happened and were still trying to make sense of it all. They staggered around the cave corridors in an uncoordinated daze.

'I know this is not the time, but we should really think about returning to Validor, just to check all is okay. Emerald is on her own out there and, after all, we do have another wedding to plan'

Pearl said this in a low voice, knowing that they all really needed time to grieve, but this was not the time or place. Ruby unlocked from Daylin's loving embrace. Ruby rubbed the tears from her cheeks.

'Yes, of course you are right. We need to see if Validor is out of darkness and Emerald has managed okay without us' Ruby said in her usual 'put others first' way.

'We would need to head back to Lightening Pass, assuming it has now returned to being the true Lightening Pass, but how would we know?' Morganite asked

'I will go first, and when I reach the other side, I will get word through Emerald that it is safe to pass through' Daylin volunteered.

'No, it's too risky Daylin, at least let me come with you' Ruby pleaded. Daylin shook his head and took both of her tiny hands into his own.

'You must trust me, I cannot tell you why right now, but I will be okay. I promise. Let's just say, I have a secret weapon if I get into trouble' he smiled earnestly trying to reassure her in his own special way.

'I will do this on my own, I know I....' and before he could finish his sentence, he found himself launched into the air, turning summersaults, until he came to a thud high above the group. He took a moment to adjust to his new surroundings, and whilst he did, the others began to laugh and scream. It was at that very moment, he realized he was sitting in his rightful place, on Nodrog's back!

Daylin gripped Nodrog's neck with both hands and tilted forward, planting a big soggy kiss on Nodrog's protruding giant cheek bones. He was gasping with sheer joy.

'It's really you, but how, I mean, I don't understand?'

Nodrog gave a toothy smile and was joined by a forlorn Dotty wearing a look of total unconditional love. Her eyes sparkling with happiness and her long eyelashes batting up and down with the sheer emotion of the situation.

'All I can say is, one minute he was dead, the next minute he was awake. It is a total miracle' winked Moonstone at Morganite. Not revealing for one second the fact that she had just performed a series of White Witch magic spells involving bolts of lightning on Nodrog which had eventually brought him back to life. All the others except Daylin, Dotty and Nodrog himself had guessed at what had happened. They were not totally confident Moonstone could do it. After all, she had never been asked to bring a Dragon back to life before, but they knew, if she could, she would.

'Okay, well I must correct myself. I will not be travelling alone, my amazing friends Nodrog and Dotty will join me on my journey back to VALIDOR'

Daylin shouted excitedly. Repeatedly kissing Nodrog over and over. Nodrog blinking with the pleasurable shock of each one, and still blissfully unaware, that for a short time, he had passed away.

CHAPTER 18

ONE PERFECT DAY

The sun smiled on everyone as they entered the sky-high turrets of the Dragon Empire, it lit up the Palace walls showing a million emeralds twinkling excitedly from the jewel encased walls. Walls which dated back to prehistoric time. A time when Dragons might have been acceptable. Creatures in those days were of a similar size and shape it would have been easy for Dragons to blend in. Who knows, maybe dinosaurs were descendants of the Dragons themselves or vice versa. Ruby looked herself up and down in the outsized ornate mirrors of the Dragon Palace. Everything was so much bigger here, she understood why it would be so, but it did look a little ostentatious at times, especially as she was such a petite female herself. She shook her dress to free it from any potential creases which would spoil its overall look. It seemed like years since they had returned to Validor to six months of long festivals and street parties held in celebration of their liberation from the Sable Witches, yet it had only been six months, and there she was, standing in her wedding dress only minutes away from becoming Daylin's wife. Everyone had made a special trip to be there. Some White Witches never had the pleasure of visiting the Dragon Empire in their entire lifetime (which was a very long time in comparison to human years), even the Mummy and his family had joined the wedding party. The Dragon Empire was a private Empire, outsiders were not always welcome. This is how they kept their residence safe from harm. That said, it would be a very brave being who ventured into such a place. This is where the most powerful magic existed. Magic beyond that of any Sable or White Witch capability and although that made Ruby feel safe, she did not feel like she fit into the Dragon way of life just yet, but she knew she and Daylin were destined to be together, and this was meant to be.

'Do I look okay mother?' Ruby asked, feeling a little overwhelmed by the whole event.

'Ruby, you look stunning. You must enjoy every minute of your day; wedding days go so very quickly'

Ruby nodded, still looking a little unsettled.

'What is it Ruby, is something bothering you?' Amber asked caringly.

'Yes, I mean, well, you know how Daylin must transform into a Dragon for the ceremony. Well, what if that scares me and well...'

'My darling, he is still Daylin, you will feel his presence, even if his image has changed. It will still be Daylin'

Ruby gave a firm nod, a look of relief spreading like a ripple of water across her face. Her mother always knew how to say the right thing's and today was no exception. Amber continued to straighten Ruby's veil and twinkling diamond crown, knowing that any more words would be over re-assurance to Ruby and make her more uncomfortable. She knew her daughter. The clock chimed midnight, an unusual time for a human wedding, but in the Dragon Empire, this was the only time you could get married. Ruby headed down the long wooden paneled corridor, passing the pictures of Dragons of former Empires and curtseying each painting as she passed. She tapped the doorway of each of the White Witches bed chamber on the way in, as she did, each one of them emerged, one by one, walking single file behind Ruby. They whispered and murmured excitedly in her path, but Ruby was oblivious to it, the butterflies in her stomach were dancing a rapid tango at this point. She stayed focused on not tripping on her dress as she descended the white marble staircase, and gripping the black onyx banister rail, she took light steps down each one until she reached the bottom, the start of the Aisle. The Aisle was at least seventy feet long and a long walk in such a heavy dress, plenty of time for an accidental trip, and just as the thought entered her head, she felt herself falling forward. Her shoe had become tangled in embroidery at the front of her dress. Then quick as a flash she was upright once more. She glanced backwards to check she understood what had just happened. Then she saw Pearl give her a knowing wink. *Thank you Pearl* she muttered under her breath. Pearl had worked some seriously quick magic to reverse time, only she and Ruby would ever know this, Ruby was so very appreciative. She mouthed the words 'thank you' to Pearl. Pearl mouthed back 'I got you' It was Pearls newest White magic, it had taken an eternity to learn, but she finally got it. She reached the end of the aisle and waited. It was traditional in Dragon Empire for the bride to await the groom. Then, there he was, standing right in front of her. He was a tower of gold, his scales almost glowing in the light of the Palace. Ruby froze for half a second. Daylin did the same, as if he was allowing her to digest what she was seeing. Charles squeezed her hand who was standing on the left of her. Daylin had appeared from a trapdoor on her right, he was not fully exposed, only his head shoulders and torso bringing him to the same height as her, and, as big and as Dragon like as his head was, his eyes met hers. It was then she saw him, his eyes may have been much larger, but they were still the enchanting loving green eyes she had met at the Stream of Undying Love, so very long ago. She touched the end of his nose with her hand, letting him know that everything was okay.

The officiant was another Dragon who stayed behind the alter at a distance, and prior to starting the ceremony, he lit each candelabra with a stream of fire from his mouth. This was the sacred fire of the holy Dragon; it was meant to bring magic which helped a Dragon marriage last for all eternity. Moonstone had also brought her own decorations, a series of bauble like lights floating around the wedding party as the loving couple said each Dragonian vow, in the language of the Dragons Unbeknown to most, the lights were other new White Witches which had wanted to join the ceremony, but numbers were limited, so Moonstone used her magic to transform them into the lights she often used to travel in secret across Validor. She had thought herself quite ingenious, but overlooked the fact that Dragons knew everything, but had allowed her to continue. They knew exactly who the lights were and were keeping a close eye on the wedding gate crashers. The White Witches may be new and harmless, but a little magic in the wrong hands, often lead to disaster and they were very much aware of that.

The last vow was uttered as Daylin and Ruby were pronounced Dragon and Wife. This was immediately followed by the final blessing, the procession of past Dragon Emperors each giving a magical gift to Ruby and Daylin. The gifts came in all shapes and sizes, many of them a total puzzle to Ruby, but she followed Daylin's lead who was taking it all in his (very large) stride and seemed to know what each gift meant. Ruby knew she needed to do some real brushing up on Dragon history during her marriage, things may then start to make a little more sense. After the last former Emperor had exited the side door of the palace. There was a thunderous roar from all the Dragons present. Ruby clasped her ears; the noise was deafening but it quickly came to a stop. Allowing the claps and cheers of the White Witches to take over. Amber and Charles gave Ruby a loving hug and in the time that she was distracted, Daylin had returned to his former appearance and was holding Ruby, both hands around her waist and whispering

'I love you my Empress'

'I love you too my Emperor' She smiled; both of their eyes filled with absolute adoration.

CHAPTER 19

WHITE SWAN LAKE

The years passed by and Daylin and Ruby never failed to be happy. The former Empress Amphi and Emperor Anthros became their closest friends and confidents. They had now abdicated to allow Daylin to take his rightful place on the throne with his new wife beside him. They knew what it was to carry the weight of all the responsibility of the Dragon Empire, and were forever at their side, helping where they could. They were surrounded each day with many people who really supported them as rulers of the Dragons. They were known to be fair and caring. A compassionate team, which is something that had been lacking in their predecessors for some time. They were respected for all that they did for the Dragon Empire and when they were eventually blessed with a beautiful daughter who they named Buttercup. It was as though the universe was thanking them for all that they had done for their (not so little) corner of it. Buttercup was a very gifted girl who knew instinctively how to guide and teach children. Her mission was to prepare them for all that life would bring and make them the best version of themselves. As an adult this became Buttercups true vocation, and she was incredibly good at it. People sent their children millions of miles, sometimes from other realms to learn from Buttercups unmatched wisdom. She had inherited all the good values of her mother and father and used them extensively to help children of all types, as well as the little Dragons of her own community. As such, it was not long before she started to receive the admiration of the males in her community, and when she eventually reached the age when a Dragon female would typically marry. Her parents watched on, as suitor after suitor tried to win her heart, but alas, Buttercup was not easily distracted from her work, that was until she met the blond haired, blue eyed Androno, a boy who also worked his own kind of magic with children, a kindred spirit, the yin to her yang. An opposite in terms of masculinity and femininity, but equally matched by their pure and good intentions for all the people that they met. Their passion for their work, quickly transforming into a strong love and bond between each other. Until the inevitable day came, the day Androno asked her mother and father for her hand in marriage. Ruby and Daylin did not hesitate to give their blessing, both had known for a long time that they could not find a kinder more loving man for their only daughter.

Amber and Charles stood next to their granddaughter and now new grandson, smiling from ear to ear throughout the spectacular wedding. It took place in the palace grounds. It was a large affair in the open air, surrounded by butterflies and every child the glamourous couple had ever helped. Everyone watched as the inseparable two of them exchanged their vows. It was a truly special day. Except for one thing, Charles and

Amber were harboring a very sad secret from the family. Amber had become very sick in recent weeks, and she had waited so long for the right moment to tell her daughter and son in law. After the guests dispersed and the happy couple disappeared into the shadows. Amber plucked up the courage to reveal exactly how sick she had become, she felt she had kept it from them for far too long. Ruby's heart was broken, she was absolutely crushed to the core by the news from her mother. Visibly shaken she dropped into her seat. She could not believe that life could be so cruel. She knew her mother did not have the powers of a White Witch and had no real chance of fighting her illness with internal magic. Ruby knew she had no choice but to return to earth to be close to her mother in her later years. She discussed it night after night with Daylin. She even called to Moonstone for help, but Moonstones powers had faded over the years, and she was sure she would not be able to help any more. She called on Morganite, now a very old man, whose powers had grown weaker over time. The new White Witches had not learned enough to build the magic specialisms Morganite, or Moonstone once had. The fateful day came when Buttercup returned from her honeymoon, elated with her new life, to be abruptly faced with a reminder of the darker side of life. Crumbling into her mother's arms, she thought she might never stop crying, of course she understood that her mother must leave and help back on earth, she supported her decision whole heartedly, but it did not help with the excruciating pain inside her chest she felt each time she thought of losing her loving Grandmother. What made things considerably worst was that she had to be without her parents so soon after her own wedding day, but she knew this was the way things should be, Ambers need for her mother was greater than her own right now. It was only a matter of days after Buttercup returned, that Ruby and Daylin leaving for earth. It gave them little time to prepare Buttercup and Androno for their new life. Their new life as temporary

Emperor and Empress of the Dragon realm. They spent the last few days with them in the palace library with all their top professors, giving Androno and Buttercup lessons in Dragonian Law. Buttercup would leave the library each night, physically and mentally exhausted. Androno would cosset her in his arms and carry her up the palace stairs. The day come for Ruby and Daylin to leave. They made their goodbyes short and sweet, exchanging small kisses on each cheek. Daylin rapped a White velvet cloak around Ruby's shoulders and lifted the hood over her head, keeping her in disguise for her journey back to earth.

CHAPTER 20

THE CROWN

A whole two years past so quickly, Ruby and Daylin had found an old railway station house to live in close to the sea. It was surrounded by the healing powers of the sea. Every day Ruby would read the spell books and practice with the Ruby in the hope that she could replicate the magic Moonstone had once been able to create, the power to bring something back to life, the power to nurse something back to full health. Either of those magical spells would be all that Ruby could wish for, but the one thing that seemed to be eluding the White Witches at the exact time that she needed it most. Ruby became completely preoccupied with this desire to make her mother better, she forgot about everything and everyone else around her. She studied and practiced day and night and didn't leave her house. Dirty pots and dishes stacked everywhere, bubbling potions, each day trying something new, in-between feeding and changing her rapidly deteriorating mother. Daylin would patiently move around her, ghost like, cleaning up the chaos, but saying nothing. It saddened him to see his wife this way, but he knew this was what she needed to do, and he was not going to try and get in her way.

A new day came, and Ruby started it in the same way as she had every other for the past two years. Fixing her mother's porridge, mixing in a concoction of healing herbs from the garden. Walking it up the stairs and spoon feeding her mother whilst Charles sat close by. Reading her mother, a chapter from a book, then returning the dish back to the kitchen, but today was going to be a different day. As she began to rinse the used cereal bowl, there was a bang on the back door. It was the sound of knuckles rattling against the glass. She wiped her hand and tentatively opened the door. She almost fell over when she saw who was standing there. It was Buttercup and Androno and cradled in Buttercups arms was a beautiful newborn baby.

'Hello Mother, I would like you to meet my daughter Primrose!'

Ruby dropped the tea towel to the floor and burst into tears of joy, gesturing to Buttercup that she would love to hold Primrose but still unable to speak through her tears. Daylin smiled and took Primrose from Ruby's arms and passed her to Ruby. He had been aware that Buttercup was coming but had been unable to distract Ruby from her research for long enough to let her know. All he knew was that this is something which would do both Ruby and her mother the power of good. It was only after they had been cooing and laughing for nearly two days those things settled down and the serious conversations began. Prior to that, they took Primrose for summer night walks around the lake, sat in the garden drinking tea together. They told the funny story about the day Primrose was born and how Daylin rode on horseback to the hospital in only his underwear. Amber was even able to get out with a walking stick and stroll along the country road with them. It took every drop of stamina she had but it was something she really did not want to miss, whatever the situation.

It was the last night before Buttercup and Androno were preparing to return to the Dragon Emperor when the conversation turned a very unexpected direction. Buttercup perched on the sofa with her mother, Daylin and Charles. Amber was fast asleep; she was not awake beyond six pm in the evening these days.

'Mother, there is something I need to ask you. My visit has a more important reason that just catching up I am afraid' Buttercup said nervously. Androno touched her arm, as if to say, *it's okay, I am here, we can do this.* Ruby nodded, looking across the three faces to try and work out what type of news they were about to deliver to her.

'Really, I mean, is everything okay?'

'Yes, well no. There is a really big favour I need to ask you mother and you Father'

Daylin sat up in his chair, wanting to pay attention. He was always there for anything his family needed and he wanted to be sure they knew that.

'Of course, you know we will help with anything we can, all you need to do is ask?'

Buttercup glanced at Androno once more, Androno nodded as if to say, carry on.

'Mum, Dad, I would like Primrose to live here with you. I realise you cannot come back and look after things in the Dragon Empire just yet, and the ideal would be that we could stay here with Primrose, but that just isn't possible'

Ruby lifted one hand in the air as if to silence Buttercup for a moment.

'Wait, I do not understand, why would you want to leave Primrose here on earth?'

Buttercup put her head in her hands, becoming extremely emotional at the thought of leaving Primrose. Androno stepped in to explain.

'There is a war in our Dragon Empire, and we cannot risk losing Primrose. We both feel she would be safer here'

'We just need a little time to bring things under control for the whole empire that is all' Buttercup chipped in.

Daylin spoke first.

'Well of course, yes, she can stay here as long as you need. You can visit whenever you are able, and we will keep in contact as best we can, wont we Ruby?' Daylin implored.

Ruby was staring into space in a trance like state.

'Ruby, we can have her, can't we?' Daylin asked again. Ruby began to mentally return to the room.

'Yes, yes of course. I just wish there was more that we could do'

Buttercup nodded and gave a tight smile.

'I know mum, it's hard for all of us, but this is the best way. At least for now.'

Ruby nodded robotically once more, she was sure she would wake up any minute and find she had been dreaming the whole disastrous chain of events. All she could do is give Primrose a safe place to stay for as long as she needed it, but for every day Primrose was with them, Amber's health began to improve, she grew stronger and stronger. Ruby could not believe her eyes, Amber and Primrose racing around the garden together, dancing with the butterflies. The garden filled with laughter and high spirits every day. Nights turned into weeks, weeks turned into months, months turned into years. Precisely, thirteen years, thirteen months, thirteen days and thirteen seconds to be precise had since the day when Primrose came to stay.

CHAPTER 21

THE BROKEN SPELL

Ruby could not fight the notion that Emerald, and Sapphire had been quite right, despite the fact that it may have been the alcohol in the wine making them speak rather too directly with her. It was time that Primrose knew who she truly was. Buttercup and Daylin had agreed to be there to ensure the day went smoothly. Daylin, and Amber, were preparing the garden for their special guests, Amber still keen to help with the White Witch Sept Ceremony for her own Great Granddaughter. It would be the ceremony which showed Primrose who she was, and the family of White Witches she had been born into. Ruby remembered the day so well herself; it was such a special night that seemed only minutes ago, yet it had been nearly thirty-five years since. Although, it wasn't quite the same for Primrose. Ruby had a slower more measured introduction to the world of witching, whereas Primrose, well she was very different. Far more special, with much more superior powers. She was a White Witch, but she was also the daughter of an Emperor and Empress of the Dragons. That was unheard of, and with powers such as she had (and will have), she will become a target for all the evil in this world, in Validor and in the Dragon Empire. Yet there she sat, playing with the butterflies in the garden, her blond golden curls swinging across her pale white skin in the sunlight. As innocent as the day she was born, or so they thought.

Everything was in place, the music, the food, the magic goblets, the crystal bath, magic candles, everything Ruby had remembered her mother doing for her when she first became a White Witch. It had been coordinated to perfection. Androno and Buttercup arriving and placing their gifts down in the kitchen. Emerald and Sapphire were busily buzzing around. They had joined them the night before. They all gathered in the kitchen, giving one another a knowing nod, before marching out into the garden, each taking a position in a semi-circle directly behind Primrose.

'Primrose, there is something we need to tell you, something that could change your whole life, but I do not want you to be afraid, your family will help you every step of the way' said Buttercup, using all the skills she had learned through years bundled into one breath. She knew how hard this would be for Primrose to comprehend and she wanted to be the one to get her own daughter threw this major transition in her life.

Primrose turned around and the butterfly's magically formed a perfect circle around her head like a multicolored crown floating around and around in a butterfly halo. Primrose began to speak in a manner way beyond her years. It was the voice of a true leader coming from the mouth of a babe.

'Please do not worry mother, I know, I have known for a long time, the butterflies have been visiting me in the garden for nearly a year now and teaching me magic. They swore me to secrecy up until now. They have trained me and guided me, showing me so much love and magic. They even made Grandmother better!'

Ruby gasped, Buttercup looked at Androno, then her father, her mouth flapping open and shut at an absolute loss for words. She continued.

'It is you who needs to be ready. I know, I am destined to be the new Queen of Validor, I also know that I am the only one who can end the war in the Dragon Empire. I am ready and it is time. Grandma, please pass me the Ruby' she asked with the voice as smooth as silk, like that you would imagine an angel to have. Ruby took the Ruby from her pocket and passed it to Primrose. Primrose investigated the Ruby as if confirming her worst suspicions, then continued with her speech.

'I also know, that as of ten seconds ago, the Sable Witches were released from your Ruby Grandmother. The magic has worn off, you all knew it would not last forever. I have no time to lose. I need to get my cloak.

She rose to her feet, almost majestically.

'It is time to save us all before it is too late'

THE END

Printed in Great Britain
by Amazon